The out

Elizabeth paused in front of the table of books, her attention drawn to a book lying open, *Rogues Across Time*. She stared at the black-and-white sketch of a man's angular face. He wore a hat and his eyes were light-colored. He seemed to be looking at her, which of course she knew was ridiculous. Elizabeth tried to turn away but found her fingers tracing the lines on the smooth pages instead.

"Is there anything in particular you're interested in?" A bearded man peered over the glass counter, a copy of *Sports Illustrated* in his hand.

"I'm not sure yet." The book was warm to her touch, as if someone had been holding it before she entered the antique shop. She flipped open the pages. She saw pictures of famous men throughout history, but none as interesting as the cowboy or gunslinger or whatever he was.

There was something about the old book that drew her to it. Elizabeth carefully studied the sketch once again. What had made a man like this become a cold-blooded killer? What choices had he made that led to his face on a wanted poster, his life worth $15,000 in gold?

Suddenly, gunfire rang out....

Dear Reader,

Time travel? Outlaws? And Harlequin Temptation? Sure, why not? The whole concept was a pretty irresistible combination, especially to an author who usually writes humorous love stories with pets and children as secondary characters.

I admit to living a peaceful existence. The only black leather in my closet is a handbag. I've never received a speeding ticket or broken the law. And I've always been attracted to clean-shaven "nice guys," not scruffy criminals bent on avoiding arrest. I've never had the overwhelming urge to "tame" a guy who lives on the wild side. I don't think I even knew what the wild side *was*.

But after writing this book, now I know. And if I had a chance to drop into 1886 and spend some time riding with Logan Younger, robbing trains, burning biscuits, carrying a rifle, running from the law and making love in abandoned mining shacks, well, I would go. In a minute.

Wouldn't you? I hope you'll read *The Cowboy* and find out for yourself.

Love,

Kristine Rolofson
c/o Harlequin Temptation
225 Duncan Mill Road
Don Mills, Ontario M3B 3K9
Canada

Kristine Rolofson
THE COWBOY

Harlequin Books

TORONTO • NEW YORK • LONDON
AMSTERDAM • PARIS • SYDNEY • HAMBURG
STOCKHOLM • ATHENS • TOKYO • MILAN
MADRID • WARSAW • BUDAPEST • AUCKLAND

ISBN 0-373-25669-8

THE COWBOY

Copyright © 1996 by Kristine Rolofson.

This edition published by arrangement with Harlequin Books S.A.

® and TM are trademarks of the publisher. Trademarks indicated with
® are registered in the United States Patent and Trademark Office, the
Canadian Trade Marks Office and in other countries.

Printed in U.S.A.

ROGUES

Rogues Across Time

THE COWBOY

Outlaws and gunslingers were a rough breed of men, dangerous and yet often revered by those around them. These Western outlaws inspired awe, fear and a grudging respect wherever they roamed. Men like Jesse James, Billy the Kid, Wyatt Earp and Wild Bill Hickock lived by the gun and died by the gun, no matter what side of the law they were on.

Logan Younger was a notorious train robber in the 1880s. He terrorized the Southern Pacific Railroad for several years, until the price on his head reached $15,000. A cousin to the infamous Younger brothers of Kansas, Logan is said to have spent several years incarcerated in California. Wanted for murder in the state of Utah and surrounding Territories, Younger and his gang stole more than $80,000 in gold from the railroads before their reign of terror ended.

1

THE OUTLAW CALLED to her. Elizabeth paused in front of the table of books, her attention drawn to a book lying open. She stared at a black-and-white sketch of a man's angular face. He was wearing a hat and his eyes were light colored. He seemed to be looking at her, which of course she knew was ridiculous. Elizabeth tried to turn away, but found her fingers tracing the lines on the smooth pages instead.

"Is there anything in particular you're interested in?" a bearded old man asked as he peered over the glass counter, a copy of *Sports Illustrated* in his hand.

"I'm not sure yet." The book was warm to her touch, as if someone had been holding it before she entered the antique shop. She flipped the pages forward to the cover page, but the author's name was obliterated by a stain. The price, twenty-five dollars, was scrawled in pencil in the corner. Thankfully, there was no dedication or owner's name inside the cover. She could erase the price and write in "Richardson" without a problem. As she thumbed through the book, she saw pictures of famous men throughout history, but none as interesting as the outlaw or gunslinger or whatever he was. The light was too dim to read, so she closed the book. *Rogues Across Time* was etched in gold lettering across the weathered brown cover. She picked up the book and tucked it under her arm.

She continued to stroll through the crowded aisles of Utah Antiques. These were the places she liked best, the stores that piled things together in dusty jumbles. She'd found her best photographs in places like these, tucked inside black-paged albums or framed in silver.

Another display of old books in an oak case caught her eye, along with a large gold-edged platter that matched those she'd "inherited" from a fictional aunt. Two of the books were Zane Grey editions she'd never seen before, so she plucked the books from the shelf and added them to her pile of treasures.

"Any books over there are three for ten dollars," the bearded man called. "Or four dollars apiece. Take your time," he added, disappearing behind the counter. She heard the chair creak as the old man returned to his reading.

Elizabeth Richardson collected old things. Not as a hobby. And not because she had such an interest in history, either. Over the years, since she'd been able to afford to buy finer-quality antiques, she'd developed quite a collection of odd memorabilia. Her "family heirlooms," she thought wryly. She looked down at the weathered book she'd found first. *Rogues Across Time* looked old enough so she could say it belonged to her great-grandfather.

Whoever he was.

"I'VE NEVER UNDERSTOOD the appeal of the West," John stated over the phone later that evening.

"I thought you'd never been to Utah," she said, sitting cross-legged on the bed. She'd polished off a hamburger and fries from room service and nursed the rest of her diet cola while telling John about her day.

He ignored the comment. "I've made arrangements for our wedding trip," he declared. "I won't be able to take as much time off as I originally planned," he cautioned. "But we should enjoy ourselves."

"Where?" She held her breath. London, Rome, Paris were all places they'd discussed. Which one would it be?

"New York," he declared, sounding pleased. "We can stay at my uncle's apartment and see a show or two."

"I like hotels," she said. "I'd prefer a nice, anonymous private hotel room, John. And why New York? You're there every other week on business." Elizabeth caught herself, hoping he wouldn't hear the disappointment in her voice.

"We won't have to worry about jet lag," he explained. "We only have four days, and I really shouldn't take off that much time right now."

"Four days." She'd assumed they'd have at least a week.

"We'll go to Europe in the fall, Elizabeth, if you insist. Honestly, Europe is not what it used to be."

She refrained from pointing out that she didn't have anything to compare it to. Somehow, she was certain she wouldn't find touring Europe the least bit disappointing. "All right," she agreed. "New York it is."

"We'll shop," he promised. "And I'll make sure to have tickets to the ballet."

Shopping wasn't a bribe. John loved to shop. He had perfect taste, too, knowing instinctively what styles would look best on her. In the past year, she'd begun to rely on his opinions. "All right," she agreed slowly. After all, Paris would still be there in September. She'd waited this long; she could wait a few more months. And besides, wouldn't anyplace for a honeymoon be wonderful as long as she was with the man she loved?

"Good girl," he said, sounding pleased. "When do you return? Do you want me to send the car for you?"

"I'd love it. I'll be in Boston tomorrow evening, at 7:10 on United Airlines."

"Gregory will be there," John promised. "I'll still be at the office, but call me when you get in and we'll see about meeting for a late dinner."

"I'll catch a nap on the plane," Elizabeth said, grinning as she picked up her glass of cola. A "late dinner" meant sex and sandwiches at her apartment. They had little privacy at his town house, since Mark and Sharon were constantly in and out. She hoped that would change after the wedding. She liked her future stepchildren, but sometimes they had little regard for other people's feelings. She was sure that would change after the wedding.

"Fine," John said. "I'll see you tomorrow then."

"'Bye," she whispered into the receiver. "I miss you." But he'd already broken the connection. Oh, well, she thought, hanging up the phone and replacing it on the bedside table. John wasn't romantic, but that was something she'd grown accustomed to. He admired her for her ability to make his life run smoother, so that's what she did. What she would continue to do. True, it wasn't the most romantic relationship, but it was a lot more than most marriages were built on. Friendship, compatibility and pretty good sex was nothing to sneeze at. But sometimes she wished he would surprise her with flowers or kiss her passionately in the middle of the opera. She wished he would look at her as if he couldn't get enough of her.

Foolish romantic wishes were not something she let herself indulge in. She was a very lucky woman, she reminded herself. Elizabeth nibbled on a cold French fry and reached for the remote. She needed noise to fill the loneliness.

Her wedding was to take place next month. In twenty-four days, she would be Elizabeth Lovell, wife of Boston Hospital's most skilled and well-known heart surgeon. She would step into a social whirl that included Christmas in Aspen with John's illustrious family. She would chair charitable fund-raisers, serve on the board of the Boston Symphony and organize her husband's home life so he would never have to worry about a thing. She would move into the elegant Lovell mansion and proceed to entertain John's office staff, friends and grown stepchildren.

Elizabeth was good at organizing things. She liked things neat and perfect, including herself. She'd learned early on that if you were perfect, then nothing bad could happen. No one would reject you or throw your meager possessions into a garbage bag and call a social worker to pick you up.

And here she was in Salt Lake City, when she should have been in Boston. Once she returned to Boston, only three weeks remained until the wedding. She hadn't wanted to come to Utah, although the annual conference for clinic management was usually enjoyable. And since her future mother-in-law had taken over the wedding plans, there wasn't much to do. Everything was in Evelyn Lovell's capable and tasteful hands. After all, John was their only son, and even though this was his second marriage there were still appearances to uphold.

And appearances were everything. Elizabeth couldn't agree more. Her unruly brunette curls were tamed to a neat shoulder-length bob and her petite frame was usually draped in classic suits and smooth

hose. There was nothing about Elizabeth Richardson
that would cause suspicion or embarrassment. Evelyn
had coaxed her into purchasing an ivory suit, stating
that the opulent satin and beaded wedding gown they
saw at the bridal department was too ostentatious for
a second wedding, especially since the groom had
grown children. Elizabeth would die before she was
ostentatious, although she cast the elegant gown a
covetous look before following her future mother-in-
law to a different section of the store.

The view from her window stretched past clean
buildings and up to distant mountains with jagged
peaks topped with snow. There had even been time off
to explore the shops a little, although she'd debated
whether or not she wanted the expense of renting a car
and exploring the country. The mountains were beautiful. They made her want to get behind the wheel of a
fast car and drive all day.

She moved away from the window and turned on the
television for company. There was something about the
old book on the dresser that drew her to it. She'd packed
the other westerns along with the rest of her luggage,
but *Rogues Across Time* was too interesting to pack
without looking through it. She wasn't tired, not really, and she'd read enough about health-care management in the nineties to last a lifetime. So she put on her
nightgown, switched off all the lights except for the one
by her bed and scooted under the covers, the book
propped on her stomach. She ignored the odd vibration that seemed to emanate from the pages, dismiss-
ing it as something that was coming through the floor
from below.

She turned the pages carefully, skimming over the
descriptions of intriguing kinds of men in history, until

the sketch of the rough-looking Western man once again fascinated her. She blinked against a sudden dizziness and closed her eyes until the sensation passed. It had happened before, especially during times of stress.

Elizabeth concentrated on the book and waited for her head to clear. The sketch showed a wanted poster. According to the poster, this outlaw had killed six men. The Southern Pacific Railroad was tired of being robbed and offered a reward of fifteen thousand dollars in gold for his apprehension. He looked cold and forbidding, with his straight lips and high cheekbones, the Marlboro Man with a bad attitude.

The article underneath gave a brief description of the outlaw life. Gunslingers, gamblers, train robbers, cattle rustlers all came under the heading. The article began:

Outlaws and gunslingers were a rough breed of men, dangerous and yet often revered by those around them. These Western outlaws inspired awe, fear and a grudging respect wherever they roamed. Men like Jesse James, Billy the Kid, Wyatt Earp and Wild Bill Hickok lived by the gun and died by the gun, no matter what side of the law they were on.

Elizabeth carefully studied the sketch once again. What had made a man like this become a cold-blooded killer? What choices had he made that led to his face on a wanted poster, his life worth fifteen thousand dollars in gold?

Suddenly, gunfire rang out, startling her. She looked over at the television and watched men on horseback about to rob a train. She watched for a minute, enjoying the old movie starring Paul Newman and Robert

Redford as Butch Cassidy and the Sundance Kid. She left the book open to the page titled "Outlaws of the American West" and dropped it on the blanket before switching out the bedside light. She propped her pillows so she could lie flat and not miss any of the movie, but she couldn't resist holding the book on her lap and glancing at the sketch of the outlaw from time to time as the warmth of the old book seeped into her body.

Thirty minutes later, she realized what was missing from her life.

SHE WOKE when the morning sun touched her face. Curled in a fetal position, the covers snugly over her shoulder, Elizabeth didn't open her eyes right away. She reached for the remote, hoping to find it and turn off the noise. Sleeping with the television on was nothing new. She liked the noise; she liked the company.

She wondered if she'd remembered to set her alarm. She wondered what time it was. It didn't matter, she thought with a contented sigh. Her plane didn't leave until one. The morning was free. She could be a slob and lie in bed for hours. She could order breakfast and watch "Regis and Kathie Lee" and "Northern Exposure" reruns.

Her arm stretched across the bed until it touched John's bare back. Funny. Except for that night at the Cape last summer, John never slept naked.

So she wasn't still in Utah. Elizabeth tried to remember where she was: John's home or her apartment. She knew she had to open her eyes, but she was so warm and comfortable. It must be Saturday, since John had spent the night.

She snuggled closer to his warmth, expecting to inhale the scent of Safari. Instead, she smelled soap, and a faint trace of leather. Her eyes flew open to see a wide, muscled back inches away from her nose. Definitely not John. Definitely not Boston. The sheets were dingy white, not covered with Laura Ashley flowers. The man wasn't wearing "Safari" or have wavy blond hair.

There was a strange man in bed with her in her Marriott Hotel room. A man whose dark hair was too long. A man whose shoulders were too wide. Elizabeth kept her breathing quiet, though she thought her heart would pound out of her chest. She eased carefully away from him, praying that he wouldn't wake.

She needn't have worried. He slept like a dead man.

She hurried to the chair where she'd laid out her clothes, and prepared to grab her purse and run out the door for help, but the upholstered pink chair was no longer there.

In fact, neither were her clothes. Or the television. Or anything except a double bed with a sleeping man in it. The room was smaller, the open window small-paned with simple lace curtains blowing in the breeze. This wasn't the impersonal, modern room at the Marriott. This place, with its wooden floor and painted walls was old and needed a good scrubbing.

How on earth had she gotten here? Had she been drugged and kidnapped in the middle of the night? Elizabeth looked down to see that she was still wearing her long-sleeved blue nightgown. She spun around, anxious to get to the door. Wherever she was, there must be people out there who could help.

"Hold it, sweetheart," a low voice ordered. She turned around slowly as the man propped himself up on one elbow and adjusted the revolver in his hand. He yawned, but the gun in his hand remained pointed at her heart. "You going or coming?"

"Going." She hid her terror, lifted her chin and dared him to argue. It was a look that worked beautifully at board meetings.

"Not yet." He gestured with the nose of the gun, motioning her away from the door. "I don't like surprises," he drawled.

"I'm not crazy about them myself." His eyes were dark, his eyebrows heavy. His skin was weathered and, except for his forehead which was a shade lighter than the rest of his face, tanned.

"What are you doing in my room?" he asked.

"You don't know?"

He smiled, or at least she thought he smiled. It was over fast. "Darlin', do I owe you something extra for last night?"

"No, you certainly don't. I need to leave now, before—" She stopped. She had no idea where she was going or where she was. She only hoped she could get a taxi before she was robbed or murdered.

His eyes narrowed. "Before what?"

He looked a little like Clint Eastwood in *Unforgiven*. Kind of scruffy and mean, with an edge to his voice and a bleak expression in his silver eyes. He was younger than Eastwood, though, with dark hair.

"Before *what*?" he repeated, sliding out of bed in one smooth motion. His body was lean and strong, with not an ounce of fat anywhere. She caught a glimpse of white buttocks as he leaned over and grabbed a pair of pants. She took the opportunity to step backward toward the door.

"Don't move," he said, seeming to have eyes in the back of his head. "What's your name? I didn't know Lottie had any new girls."

"Elizabeth," she answered without thinking. "Elizabeth Richardson."

His eyes narrowed as he stared at her. The amused light in his eyes died. "And where exactly are you from, Elizabeth Richardson?"

Her mind went blank for one paralyzing instant, until she remembered. "Boston. Massachusetts."

"Do you know who I am?"

She knew exactly who he was now. He was the man in the wanted poster, the illustration in the old book she'd bought yesterday afternoon. Which was impossible. Logan Younger was an outlaw from at least one hundred years ago. "No. I don't have any idea who you are," she lied. He knew it, too. She could tell by the way his lips thinned.

"Get back in the bed."

Elizabeth stared at him. "What?"

He glanced down at her billowing flannel gown. "That's where you were, weren't you?"

She nodded, but didn't move until he pointed the gun at her again. She did as she was told, willing her quaking knees to support her until she sank onto the mattress. He took a length of rope and tied her hands behind her back, then fastened the rope to the iron headboard. "There," he declared. "Now I don't have to worry about what you're doing and who you're talking to."

"Look," she said, "there's been some kind of mistake. It's one of those 'wrong place at the wrong time' situations. I don't know how I got here, but you have to—"

"Shut up!" He dressed quickly, pulling on a cotton shirt, worn leather vest, boots and a wide-brimmed felt hat. He checked two revolvers, added bullets and hooked a gun belt around his hips. "Lady, I am not getting killed today," he muttered. "No way."

"Well, that's fine with me, but I have a plane to catch."

He ignored her and peered cautiously out the window. "Where is he?"

"Who?"

"Don't play dumb, honey. Just tell me where he is."

"I really wish I knew who you were talking about, but I don't." She told herself to stay calm. The rope wasn't tight, just unyielding. She wasn't in pain, although she'd love to find a bathroom. She would take this one step at a time, she told herself, and, with a little luck, escape with her life. The outlaw didn't seem interested in hurting her. He was more interested in studying the street below. There was danger and he thought she was part of it. "I'm not who you think I am. Really," she added, hoping he was paying attention. She paused for a moment, then asked, "Who are you?"

"Logan Younger, ma'am, at your service." He frowned again. "Do I have to gag you?" He cast a swift glance in her direction. "I'm trying to concentrate on staying alive here and your appearance in my bed is complicating the morning."

"It's not doing much for my day, either," she grumbled under her breath. She looked around the room, hoping to see something that would give her a clue as to where she was. A hotel room, obviously. One that had seen better days. A kerosene lamp stood on a table to her right, the bedclothes were rumpled and an old book lay open by her pillow. A strange chill rushed past her heart as she stared at the book. She couldn't make out the title, but she'd bet her life savings that the gold lettering on the cover spelled *Rogues Across Time*.

HE SHOULD HAVE KNOWN Al Richardson wouldn't be far behind. The Southern Pacific wouldn't take the robberies lightly. They would be furious, he thought, a satisfied smile crossing his face. Old Crocker was most likely ranting and raving from his Sacramento mansion about last month's robbery. Logan Younger and his band of outlaws would have a higher price on their heads faster than you could say "railroad," a fact that meant manhunters wouldn't be far behind. Al shouldn't have involved a woman, but the man would stop at nothing to get what he wanted.

He'd proved that years before, and Logan's life hadn't been the same since.

Logan moved away from the side of the window and crossed the room to make sure the door was locked. The woman watched every move he made. She was a pretty thing, with all that loose brown hair and eyes the color of a bluebird's wing. Sarah's shade.

He didn't like the idea of a whore having Sarah's eyes.

And he didn't want her in his bed.

He would leave her here. Richardson could find her easily enough. He didn't know what their plan had been, but it was over now. Chances are, she was to have distracted him while Al set the trap. He slept with the door barred. How in hell had she gotten in? Lottie's whiskey had more kick than he thought if he'd been hoodwinked into taking a woman up to his room. He should have known better than to let down his guard, even in a quiet Mormon town like Salt Lake.

"Please," the woman whispered. "Let me go."

He shook his head and stood at the foot of the bed. "Can't do that, sweetheart. Al will find you. Don't worry."

"Al? Who is that?"

She was a good actress, too, he noted. All wide-eyed innocence and fear. He winked at her before turning away. "Nice try."

"Logan!" came a low whisper, followed by a soft rap on the door. "You ready?"

Logan picked up his revolver and moved toward the door. "Billy?"

"Yeah, who else? Let me in. We've got some trouble brewin'."

Logan unlatched the door and opened it enough so the older man could slip inside. "Yeah. I know. I've got part of it right here in my bed."

"Holy smokes! Who is she?" Billy paused at the foot of the bed and the young woman blushed as Billy tipped his hat to her. "Howdy, ma'am."

"She's a Richardson." He didn't know why she'd blush like that. That nightgown covered as much of her as a dress would. She probably didn't like being at a disadvantage, tied up and all, no matter who she was.

"Richardson?" Billy, a robust man with a white beard and piercing gray eyes, turned his attention toward Logan. "How in hell did she wind up in here?"

He shrugged. "I don't know. We'll leave her tied up and let Richardson find her. He must be around."

"He's around, all right. Rumor has it he was in Ogden looking around two days ago. I heard he was lookin' for someone. You're gonna hafta leave town, but I wouldn't be surprised if he has more men with him and they're guardin' the hotel right now. It's awful quiet out there."

"Yeah," Logan agreed. "It's still early, though. Folks will be through town soon enough."

"I don't like this, Logan. This don't seem right." His gaze flickered to the woman as he sat down in the only chair. Logan stood by the edge of the window, careful not to be seen as he watched the street.

"What doesn't seem right, Billy?"

"Tyin' up a woman like that."

Elizabeth nodded. "My thoughts exactly. Why don't you untie me and I'll tiptoe out of here and leave you to your business."

Logan kept his gaze on the street below. "You *are* my business, sweetheart."

"Elizabeth," she corrected. "Ms. Richardson."

He turned toward her and nodded. "Miz Richardson," he said. "You took a lot of risks coming into my room. You're lucky you're still alive."

"Lucky? I went to bed in my room at the Marriott and woke up in this hellhole. This is my last business trip to Utah, believe me."

"Bounty huntin' is man's work," Billy agreed, nodding his head. "You his wife?"

"Whose wife?"

"Richardson's."

"No. I don't know anyone named Richardson and I'm not married. At least, not yet. Not until May eleventh."

Billy leaned forward. "You a Mormon?"

"No. This is my first—"

Logan groaned. "Quiet, both of you. There are men stationed in three places in front of the building and we have to figure out how to get out of here."

"The horses are saddled and ready, Logan. I tied 'em up in the back."

That wasn't going to work. If Richardson and his men had the front covered, then they certainly had the back covered, too. "They're not looking for you, Billy. At least, not yet. Tell you what," he drawled, moving away from the window and going to his pack. He withdrew a leather pouch and handed it to his friend. "You take my horse and I'll take the wagon with the supplies. Then get Miss Richardson some clothes—*big* clothes—and get yourself another shirt. I'll be wearing yours."

"You have an idea how we're gettin' out of here alive?"

Logan nodded. "Tie the wagon across the street so I can see it from here."

"Right," Billy said, tucking the pouch inside his shirt. "I'll be back as soon as I can."

Logan smiled at Elizabeth, enjoying the spark of anger that lit her blue eyes. "We're not going anywhere, are we, darlin'?"

"I'm going back to Boston," she snapped. "And you're going to hell!"

So she had a temper. He bit back a chuckle as Billy slipped out the door. If he wasn't in danger of being shot to death, he could almost enjoy himself. He moved closer to the bed and returned his gun to the holster. "Lady, you have quite a mouth on you."

"Just tell me where I am."

"You don't know?" She shook her head. "Lottie's," he explained, feeling the tiniest bit sorry for her. "It's a hotel. Right down the street is that Mormon temple they're still building."

"In Salt Lake City?"

"Yes," he said, giving her a questioning look. "It's a clean town. Respectable, for the most part."

She went quiet again, as if she was thinking. He wondered if she'd hidden a gun somewhere near the bed. If she had, then he was all kinds of fool to just be searching for it now. She could have shot him ten times over, if she'd wanted. And he was sure she did.

She didn't look too happy as he approached the bed. "What are you doing?" she asked.

"Looking for the gun."

"You lost a gun? You have two strapped to your waist. How many do you need?"

"I'm looking for *your* gun," he said, sliding his hand carefully between the mattress and the metal springs.

"I don't know how to shoot a gun."

There was nothing stashed underneath the mattress, nothing behind the pillow or tucked between the iron headboard and the wall. "Then I guess it's a good thing you don't have one," he said, sitting on the bed. His body made a dip in the mattress, rolling her toward him. She quickly wriggled away and glared at him. He didn't understand much about this morning. Was she a crazy woman? He might think so, except for her name. Yet she hadn't been smart enough to lie about that, either. "What's a Mare-iette?"

She gave him another one of those odd looks before she answered, as if she was wondering if he was making fun of her. "Marriott. A chain of hotels across the country. *Clean* hotels. Great food. Can I go to the bathroom?"

He hadn't thought of that particular problem. "Yeah. Out back."

"There isn't a bathroom in here?"

He bent down and looked under the bed. "No," he said, straightening. "You'll have to wait."

She rolled her eyes and looked up at the ceiling. "Just my luck I end up in a hotel with an outhouse. Where *am* I?"

"Utah Territory, lady." He left the bed and sidled up to the window. "I wish Billy would get that wagon."

"Utah *Territory?*" She frowned as he turned back to look at her. Her skin went pale and her eyes were wide and frightened. "What year is this?"

She was loco, all right. He'd been stuck with a loco woman in his bed just when things were going according to plan. He'd had a long time to plan this, three endless years, and now he was within days of pulling it off. "It's May 1886."

"That's impossible." Her voice was very, very soft and she stared up at him with those dark-lashed eyes.

"No, lady, it's not," he said, trying to show great patience. Thank the Lord he'd tied her up right away, before she'd killed them both. "It's 1886, and this is Utah, not a Mare-iette."

She closed her eyes and he saw her lips move as if in prayer. At least she was being quiet. She had a heart-shaped face and clear skin. If he didn't know better, he would mistake her for one of those society women touring the country by train. They enjoyed a side trip to Salt Lake to look at the Mormon men walking through town accompanied by three or four wives.

"Who's president?"

"Grover Cleveland. This some kind of test?"

She didn't look as if she believed him. "What year were you born?"

He answered to kill time. The wagon still hadn't appeared. "1856."

The woman thought that over for a minute, then seemed hesitant. "I would really like to go to the bathroom."

He debated that one. The outhouse was at the end of a short path out back, by the kitchen. He could walk her to the door, then watch her take the few steps across the fenced yard. As long as he stayed out of sight and she stayed in the outhouse, there shouldn't be any problem. Damn, he didn't want to get shot!

"If you make any noise, I'll shoot you," he promised as he stepped over to the bed, hoping to frighten her.

It worked. Her hands trembled as he untied her and she rubbed her palms together as soon as she was free. "Thank you," she said, sitting up and smoothing her nightgown. "Although things would be much easier if you just let me go."

"Go where? Where is Richardson and what are his plans?" Logan stared at her and waited. "You tell me," he urged, "and I might be able to release you."

She stared back at him and lifted her chin. "He's waiting across the street, in the, uh, bank. He's, uh, coming over here at ten o'clock."

Logan pretended to accept the information. She was lying and she wasn't very good at it. The nearest bank was two blocks west. He'd like to know how Sonny had involved her in this. He must have been desperate, and she must have been paid a lot of money, or else she was so in love with him she'd do anything. "Are you really his wife?"

"No," she snapped, then looked as if she regretted the word.

"Come on." He took her elbow and pulled out his revolver. Was this part of the setup, a way to get him out of his room and into the open?

He hoped to hell it wasn't. If she double-crossed, him he would shoot her.

2

THEY MET NO ONE in the narrow hallway. One skinny youngster, dressed in rough cowboy gear, tipped his hat when they met him on the back stairs. A woman in a calico dress, her outlandish red hair frizzed and piled on top of her head, gave her a curious look but went back to pounding bread dough on a wide wooden table in the kitchen. She didn't look as if she'd help a stranger.

They were back in the room in ten minutes.

Elizabeth Richardson had never used an outhouse. She had never walked outdoors to relieve herself. She had never had a gun pointed on her back while she did these things.

She had never lived in 1886, either, and she didn't want to stay.

Elizabeth knew she'd fallen into something that couldn't be explained. Yesterday she had a career, a fiancé and a future. This morning she had nothing. Except a book, and a rope around her wrists.

For right now, she wanted to stay alive, and with Logan Younger pointing that gun at her, she wasn't sure how much longer that would be. She'd never had a gun pointed at her before and she didn't like it. But she didn't have any choice, at least not at the moment, and if she was in some sort of strange time warp, she could wake up tomorrow in 1996. Unless this was a dream, brought on by falling asleep to the sound of Butch Cassidy's gun.

"Back in the bed," Younger ordered, releasing her elbow and pushing her toward the bed.

"Believe me," she said, "I'm no danger to you."

He didn't appear to believe her, because he tied her up once again and then went to the window. "Billy has the wagon. It won't be long now."

The knock on the door didn't surprise either one of them, although Logan made certain it was Billy and that the man was alone before he holstered his gun once again.

"I hope I got what you wanted," Billy sputtered. "I ain't never picked out women's clothing before."

Logan took the paper-wrapped bundle and opened it. He held up a large blue-and-white calico dress. "This is just fine."

Elizabeth eyed it with some doubt. She was pleased to have something to wear besides a flannel nightgown, but she could get into that dress twice and still have enough room for her briefcase. "It's not going to fit."

"It'll fit," Logan declared, tossing it on the bed.

"I bought some other things," Billy said. "Lady's things. You know. And a good pair of boots." His gaze slipped to her bare feet. "I hope I bought 'em big enough."

She curled her legs underneath her, effectively hiding her feet from the men's inspection. They weren't that big, but she'd heard women's feet had grown larger in the last hundred years. "How am I supposed to get dressed?"

"I'll wait out in the hall," Billy said, scrambling toward the door.

Logan tipped the package upside down and dumped the contents onto the bed. "Give me your shirt, Billy, and you take this one. I want to look like a working man."

Billy unbuttoned the grayish white shirt, revealing long johns and an ample beer belly. He blushed as Logan handed him the new shirt. "Thanks," he drawled. "Blue's my favorite color."

"Mine, too," Elizabeth said, wishing he didn't look so uncomfortable. For some reason, she didn't feel threatened by the middle-aged outlaw. Maybe because he was old enough to be her father. Maybe it was because he looked more afraid of her than she was of the outlaw. She eyed the odd underthings. Plain cotton drawers trimmed with a simple edging, a camisole edged with lace and a white petticoat completed the outfit. There was also a pair of white stockings and sturdy black boots.

"He forgot to get a bonnet," Logan muttered. He opened the door and gave Billy another set of instructions while Elizabeth looked at the enormous dress spread across the bed. It had a high neck and long narrow sleeves, and the edge of the hem was trimmed with navy braid. She would look like a moose in it.

Logan returned and untied her. "Put it on and hurry. The sooner we get out of here the better off we'll all be."

"Turn around, then."

"Not on your life. For all I know, you have a knife strapped to your thigh." He almost laughed at her expression. She didn't look like a woman who knew how to handle a weapon, but a man couldn't take any chances. Especially a man with a price on his head.

"If I did, I would have used it already." Elizabeth stood up and slid the pantalettes on under her nightgown and tied them at the waist. They were loose and hung to her knees. The camisole was next, so she wriggled her arms from the nightgown and managed to get the upper half of her body covered while still concealed behind the flannel. She dared a glance at Logan, who looked amused. "You could make this a lot easier if you turned around."

"Nope," he drawled. "This is better than the dance troupe that came through Fresno."

Elizabeth glared at him, then picked up the dress and slipped it over her head. She ripped her nightgown at the neck, which gave her enough room to wiggle it over her hips and down to her ankles. Then she put her arms in the sleeves and turned to Logan. "You'll have to help me with the hooks in the back."

"In a minute," he said, picking up a length of rope and the bed's only pillow. "Put this across your, uh, waist." He handed her the pillow and, catching on to his plan, she shoved the pillow inside the bodice of the dress. She took the rope and put it around her waist, then Logan took the ends and tied them together, effectively holding the pillow in place. "You're about to become a mother."

"This is a waste of time, you know." She told herself that there was nothing intimate about a man fastening the back of her dress. "There is no one out there looking for me. In fact—"

"Not bad," he interrupted, taking her by the shoulders and turning her to face him. "Once we cover up that hair, we should be able to get out of here without a problem."

"You're an optimist."

The coldness in his eyes made her take a step backward, away from his touch. "No, Lizzie, I am certainly not that."

"Lizzie?"

He shrugged. "It seems to suit you. I can't call you Elizabeth and I'm certainly not going to say Miz Richardson whenever I want your attention."

"My friends call me Elizabeth."

"I'll bet your mother called you Lizzie."

She swallowed. Hard. "You'd lose your money."

"It wouldn't be the first time, and it won't be the last," he drawled. He stepped back to look at her. "Put up your hair."

"With what?"

"You don't have any hairpins?"

"No." Unless you counted the handful scattered in the bottom of her bathroom drawer at home. She'd used them twice, once for a New Year's Eve dance and another time for a wedding. She certainly didn't travel prepared to look glamorous.

Billy knocked twice and entered, this time carefully carrying a ladies' stiff-brimmed black bonnet and black-fringed paisley shawl. "Lottie robbed me," he complained. He handed Logan a box, then his eyes widened when he saw Elizabeth. He grinned. "You've put on a little weight, ma'am."

She patted her pillow-coated abdomen. "I don't know who you're trying to fool, but I don't think it's going to work."

"Give her the bonnet, Billy." Logan nodded his approval as Elizabeth placed it on her head. "Stuff your hair inside of it, like you were wearing it up."

She did as she was told, feeling as if she was getting ready for a Halloween party. She put on the stockings as discreetly as possible, and then the boots. They were a little big, but once she laced them they felt pretty good.

The morning still had a surreal quality. She wondered if she would wake up in a minute. She wondered if she'd died in her sleep and this was a way of reliving a past life. No. She didn't believe in that. If she was in a past life, would she be trying to figure out how to return to the future?

Logan patted face powder through his dark hair, which gave him a distinguished look, while she draped the shawl over her shoulders. She would help him escape, and then she would see about getting back to Boston. Surely there was someone who would help her.

Logan added suspenders and a pair of wire-rimmed glasses. Suddenly, he looked more like a mild-mannered husband than an outlaw, especially when a long, dark coat hid the guns secured to his hips. He took her elbow and ushered her toward the door.

"If you make a move to escape, I'll have to shoot you," he whispered. "I won't like shooting a woman, but I'm going to figure you asked for it by coming here this morning and crawling into my bed. You were asking for trouble and now you're smack-dab in the middle of it."

"You don't understand," she told him, wishing he'd believe her. "I don't have anything to do with bounty hunters."

He smiled, but it was a dangerous smile. His dark eyes remained cold as he stared down at her. "Prove it, then. We're walking out of here, man and wife, on our way home. We're going to get in the wagon and head east, out of town. You're going to keep your head down and your mouth shut. If there's any shooting, drop to the ground and try to find cover."

She nodded, suddenly filled with terror.

He turned to Billy before he opened the door and spoke in a low voice, "Wait half an hour, then take my horse and ride. Head south first, in case anyone's watching."

Billy nodded and donned his hat. "I'll meet you in Devil's Slide in two days."

"Cover me until we leave town." The older cowboy nodded once again and slipped out the door.

"Wait," Elizabeth cried, turning back to the bed. "My book!"

"What book?"

"On the bed. I can't leave without it." She looked up at him, pleading. That old book was her only connection between her life before and what was happening now. She knew she'd never be able to get back to John and Boston and her job if she left it behind. "It's all I have."

He sighed, then strode to the bed and grabbed the book, shoved it in his saddlebags and took her elbow.

"Thank you," she whispered, feeling as if she'd just risked losing her life.

"Let's go." He adjusted his worn hat so the brim rode low on his forehead.

Elizabeth tied the ends of the shawl in a loose knot below her breasts. The pillow was surprisingly comfortable and made her look about six months' pregnant. The starched brim of the bonnet blocked her side vision, and the dress was too long. She gathered the skirt in her hands so she wouldn't trip and Logan, vigilant at her side, guided her down the smooth wooden stairs. They entered the lobby, attracted a few curious glances and nothing more. Elizabeth dared a glimpse around the Victorian room, noting the red Oriental rug and the dark velvet drapes. A brass spittoon sat in one corner, a wilting plant in another. She didn't know what she had expected, but she felt as if she'd walked onto a movie set. A lavish movie set.

"Steady," Logan whispered, his hand dropping to her waist. "We're going to walk outside now. Try not to look as if you're going to be murdered."

"I thought I was."

"Yeah, well. Try not to *look* it."

"Okay," she gulped.

"Smile. Look happy. You're a contented farmer's wife." She turned her head so she could see him and gave him a phony grin. He frowned. "You look like you drank a bottle of whiskey all by yourself. Better not smile."

"All right." She didn't feel like smiling when the bright sunlight hit her. She wondered when sunglasses were invented. The sharp sunlight stung her eyes and made her blink. Logan paused under the shadow of the hotel roof. She heard him take a deep breath, then he urged her forward, to walk across the wide sidewalk and onto the dusty street.

"Well, Lizzie, it looks like the wagon is going to hold up for a few more trips to town," he said, his voice easy. "I got that ticking you wanted, and some licorice whips for Danny. There's fifty pounds of flour, too. Think that will hold us?"

He sounded like such a loving husband. "Uh, yes, I guess so. Did I tell you I don't know how to cook?" She looked straight ahead as they crossed the street. She might as well have been in an old "Bonanza" rerun. Men on horseback trotted quietly along the street, while a group of women huddled near the general store. They were wearing similar bonnets and shawls and seemed content to spend time gossiping away the bright spring morning.

"Keep walking," he said, his voice pleasant. "And keep your head down. You're still too damn easy to recognize."

"Nobody around here knows me," she assured him. "You could parade me up and down this street all day and no one would know my name."

"I wouldn't bet my life on it," he muttered. The street seemed a thousand yards wide, but they were soon at the wagon. Logan helped her onto the seat and strolled around to the left side of the wagon, patting the horses' necks as if they were old friends. He acted as if he had all the time in the world. Finally, he swung himself onto the bench. He unwrapped the reins from a wooden lever, setting the horses in motion.

"Amazing," she murmured, holding on to the side of the wagon to keep from being jolted off the seat.

"Is this where I take it in the back?" He looked over his shoulder, but there was nothing in the street to indicate trouble.

"I thought gunfighters didn't shoot each other in the back."

"Yeah, sure. We're all real noble. We like dying looking at the person who shot us." He shook his head and urged the horses faster before glancing in her direction. "That bastard Richardson would kill me any way he could, then collect the reward and move on to the next man, and we both know it."

"Just because we have the same name doesn't mean—"

"I'm no fool, sweetheart. You were in my room this morning for a reason. Someone let you in. Maybe Lottie was paid off, I don't know. But someone had a plan.

There's just one problem," he said, guiding the horses away from a collision with a wagon coming in the opposite direction.

"What's that?"

"I'm not dying today."

Elizabeth clung to the side of the bench and turned away from Logan's frightening profile. He was a man who wore guns, a man who was wanted by bounty hunters. A man who had a price on his head. A man who would probably die sooner than later.

The buildings they passed on their way out of town were lined along sidewalks and fronted with trees. The town seemed to be laid out neatly, in blocks, the houses two-storied and lovely. San Francisco without the hills, that's what the town reminded her of. The people looked content and busy. No one appeared to notice that Elizabeth Richardson had dropped in from the future.

He should have listened to Billy's advice three days ago. None of this would have happened if he hadn't taken a chance and come to Salt Lake City. He'd doubted he'd be recognized in a large town. He'd planned to check for messages at the telegraph office and send a couple of his own.

Finding Danny was more important than anything else he could think of, except staying alive. Years ago he'd promised his son that he would come for him. No matter how long it took.

Last night a bath sounded good. And sleeping in a bed, for a change. And a hot meal that someone served on a thick china plate. He'd told himself he needed supplies. He'd told himself he needed information.

He hadn't admitted he'd needed a rest. Just one night to pretend he was a human being with a life that didn't consist of running, hiding, stealing and shooting. Just one night to pretend the last six years hadn't happened. To pretend he was going home to Sarah.

Billy had agreed to go with him, and now they were both in trouble, because of one blue-eyed woman.

He drove at least a mile before he spoke again. "No one's following us," he said. "I would've spotted them by now."

"What about Billy?"

"He can take care of himself." They all could, especially after four years in the Santa Clara prison.

"Isn't he a little old for an outlaw?"

"He didn't start out being an outlaw." Damn. He shouldn't have spoken to her. Now she'd think it was all right to blab all the way up the mountains.

"I didn't start out being a pregnant kidnapping victim, either," she muttered.

"Yeah," he snorted. "I forgot. You're real blameless in all of this, aren't you?"

"As a matter of fact—"

"Never mind." He adjusted the reins and the horses trotted a little faster.

"Where are we going?"

Logan didn't respond. He planned to drop her off first chance he got, but he didn't want her to think she was out of danger yet. Miss Lizzie, or whoever she was, wasn't getting out of this mess that easily. There was something strange about this whole thing, but he couldn't figure it out.

"I think I have a right to know," she said after a long moment.

Women loved to hear the sound of their own voices. "Well, where would you like to go?"

"Boston."

"You're a hell of a long way from Boston."

"I realize that."

He glanced over at her. She looked close to tears. He couldn't tell for sure, because of that bonnet, but her voice was wobbly and she sniffed, a delicate little female sound he remembered foretold the onset of weeping. "What kind of trouble are you in, Lizzie?"

"You wouldn't believe me if I told you." She wiped her eyes on the corner of the shawl. "No one would."

"Well, maybe you're right." He knew better than to pry. Sticking your nose into someone else's business was another good way to get yourself shot. Not that the woman beside him was going to shoot him, but a man on the run couldn't be too sure.

"Have you ever thought about the future?" she asked.

Every minute of the past four years. "Yeah."

"Do you ever wonder what's going to happen?"

"I try not to think about it," he lied. Finding Danny was all he ever thought about. Seeing his son again was the only thing he lived for.

"But what if you could predict the future? What if you knew what was going to happen?"

"I reckon that would be pretty damned convenient." He chuckled, beginning to relax now that they were out of town and there was no sign of trouble. "I could've used that information more than once in my life."

"The Civil War is over, right?"

She sure was a strange woman. "For almost twenty years. For lots of folks, it seems like only yesterday. Times are hard."

"And people in California have discovered gold?"

"Yes, ma'am. There've been plenty of gold strikes here in the West in the past ten, twenty years."

"I wish I'd paid more attention in history class." She sighed. "Have they discovered gold in Alaska yet or does that come later?"

"If anyone's found gold in that territory, they're keeping the news pretty quiet." Sad that such a pretty thing could be insane. He wondered how she'd lived this long. "Lizzie, do you have people to take care of you?"

It took her a long time to reply. "No." She laughed after she said it, but it was a sad sound. "I've never had anyone do that."

His stomach growled, reminding him he hadn't eaten since last night. "You hungry?"

"Starving."

"Reach around back and see if you can find some biscuits."

She did as she was told, producing a sack of biscuits and a couple of soft apples. "What do you want?"

He took a biscuit, wishing he had time to stop and brew a pot of coffee. The woman nibbled on the biscuit and looked around as they passed the outskirts of the Mormon city. "It's so organized," she said. "Even a hundred years ago."

"Brigham Young knew what he wanted, I guess," Logan agreed. He didn't know what she meant about the "hundred years" part, but it was a fine morning, no one had shot at him and the crazy woman seated beside him was at least company. Sometimes he got so damn tired of hearing his own voice. Or not hearing a voice at all.

All that was going to change, he promised himself. He took last September's apple and bit into it, appreciating the moisture. He would get rid of his passenger and move on. One more train and he would be finished.

In just three more days he would be free.

THEY SEEMED to be traveling through a wide canyon, with rounded green mountains on either side of the large expanse of sage-covered ground. They passed a large creek bringing water from the mountains to Salt Lake City. Logan explained how the Mormons had built a series of canals to irrigate the once-dry basin. Elizabeth ate her apple and removed her shawl as the noonday sun pelted down on her shoulders. "Where are we?"

"Northeast of town."

"Where are we going?" In other words, she wondered, what was going to happen next? She waited for an answer, but he took his time thinking it over.

"Well," he drawled. "I know a safe place."

"Can I get a flight, I mean *train* back East there?"

He nodded. "They'll see that you get back to the city. You can get a train to Ogden, then take the Union Pacific east or the Southern Pacific west to Sacramento."

Another thought occurred to her. "I don't have any money."

"Lady, that's not my problem."

"You kidnapped me. I'd say it's definitely your problem." She had no Visa card, no American Express. She assumed Western Union existed, but to whom would she wire for help?

"If that's true, then it's last in a long line."

"Let me borrow some, then. I'll pay you back."

"And find out where I'm living so your boyfriend can collect his money? I don't think so."

"I'll wire it to any bank you say," she promised. "I just need to get on the train." If she took the book and re-

turned to the hotel room, would she be able to find her
way back? Somehow, the book had to be the link between the two centuries. If it worked in one direction,
surely it could work in the other. She had to tell herself
that it would or she would start sobbing and never be
able to stop.

"I'll see that you get back to Salt Lake," he said, his
voice cold. "You're on your own after that. I don't doubt
you have your ways of earning money."

"I'm not a prostitute." There was a perfectly reasonable explanation why she'd awakened in his bed this
morning, but she didn't think he'd believe a story about
antique books and time travel.

"What you are or aren't is no concern of mine. You
can find yourself a husband easy enough, I'm sure." He
chuckled as he added, "Especially here in Utah Territory."

She almost had a husband. John would be wondering what had happened to her. She looked at her wrist
and realized she didn't have her watch. Tonight, she
was to return to Massachusetts. In three weeks, she was
going to be married. Everything she had dreamed her
entire life was going to start happening in three weeks.

And Logan Younger, a hardened outlaw with a dangerous attitude, was at fault. He was not going to leave
her stranded in the middle of nowhere, miles outside of
the city. He would not get away with this.

THE LOG CABIN, a welcoming trail of smoke coming
from its stone chimney, sat nestled on the side of the
mountain, facing a small valley. Elizabeth could have
swooned in relief. She'd been in the wagon for hours,
it seemed, as they covered mile after mile at a pace more
suited to walking. She'd removed the pillow an hour

ago and used it to cushion the hard wagon seat. They'd veered from the wide, well-traveled canyon road and had headed north, toward the mountains. She wondered what they were called.

They couldn't be too far away from Salt Lake and civilization, she realized. Although each step took her farther from the city, she still had the book. She still held the key to finding her way home. If they were traveling three miles an hour, she guessed they'd covered eighteen miles so far. She was as tired as if she'd pulled the wagon herself. Perspiration had pooled on her hairline, dampening the bonnet, but Elizabeth was not about to remove it. The starched brim was the only thing protecting her face from the bright Utah sun.

He'd let her cool herself once, in the waters of a creek. She'd knelt and splashed her face with water while he was refilling the canteens and watering the horses, but he wouldn't take any time to eat. They could do that in the wagon, he'd said and, with an iron grip, had hauled the horses from the creek bed.

"This is it," he said as they followed the winding road to the cabin.

Elizabeth eyed the rickety structure as a scrawny man, wearing a T-shirt and black pants, stepped onto the porch. He was accompanied by three black dogs and a barefoot child. "You're leaving me *here?*"

Logan waited until he pulled the wagon closer before answering. "Yeah."

Elizabeth gripped the wagon seat. She'd never seen a more forsaken place in her entire life. The dark-eyed man gazed at her with interest and stepped down off the porch to greet his company. "What's goin' on, Younger?" He spit a stream of tobacco and grinned. "You need horses?"

Logan tipped his hat back and wiped his forehead with his sleeve. "Among other things. Parker, can you return this wagon to Salt Lake in about four days, along with this woman?"

Parker frowned, his gaze darting back and forth between Logan and Elizabeth. "This ain't no hotel."

Logan dropped the reins and jumped down from the wagon seat. "I'd pay you well," he assured him. "The wagon *and* the woman need to get back to town, but not too soon."

The man grinned, leering up at Elizabeth for a long moment before turning back to the outlaw. "Momma died last month. I guess I could use the comp'ny."

That was enough, Elizabeth thought. She was not about to be left at the mercy of a tobacco-spitting lecher in the middle of a mountain. She turned around and rustled underneath the heavy tarp.

"Hey!" Logan's voice was sharp. "What are you doing?"

She lifted her head and smiled innocently. "I'm looking for my book. I can't leave without it."

He nodded, then turned back to the man and pulled the leather pouch from his coat. As soon as he started counting out coins, Elizabeth dug under the biscuits and found what she was looking for. She'd noticed it when she'd searched for breakfast, but there had been no opportunity to use it. And no reason. Now, she knew, pulling the rifle into her arms, there was a very good reason.

"What the hell—" Logan spotted her the minute she turned around. "Put that down! What the hell do you think you're doing?"

Elizabeth slid over and picked up the reins. She kept the rifle in her lap and pointed toward Logan. "I'm going back to Salt Lake."

Parker took a step sideways. "I ain't armed," he yelled. "I don't want nothin' to do with this."

"Tell your boy to go inside and stay there," Logan told him. "She's crazy. That rifle could go off by accident in any direction."

"Boy!" Parker called. "Git inside and tell Sissie not to come out 'til I tell 'er she ken." The boy scurried indoors and disappeared.

"Do I have your attention?" she asked, looking straight into Logan's gray eyes.

"I guess you could say that," he drawled. She wished he'd look more frightened. His right hand hovered over his gun belt.

"Put your hands up," she ordered, suspecting he could kill her in seconds. He did as he was told, but he frowned.

"This has gone far enough," he warned.

"That's exactly what I was thinking myself," she agreed. She hit the reins on the horses' rumps the way she'd watched Logan do it, and the animals moved ahead. She kept the gun pointed at Logan for as long as she could, then it became impossible to guide the team and keep her balance while propping a rifle in her lap. Her only hope was to move the horses fast enough and hope that he would hesitate before approaching her. The road looped around a set of outbuildings and headed west, back the way they came.

"Giddy-up," she shouted, moving the reins faster. "Come on, let's *go!*"

She never noticed the thump on the back of the wagon, never knew that Logan had caught up with her and climbed in behind. She felt cold steel on her neck. Warm breath tickled her cheek as he told her to stop the team.

"Damn," she whispered, wondering if he would kill her now. She'd held a gun on him; she'd stolen his horses.

She'd read that men were hanged for less.

3

"STOP THE TEAM," he ordered, "before you kill us both."

She pulled on the reins, which was harder to do than she expected. The horses eventually slowed and then stopped. Elizabeth held her head still, certain she would be dead in an instant if she fought him.

But what if she was already dead—had died in her sleep, a brain aneurism or something sudden—at the Marriott. This could be one of those dips into another lifetime the spirit experienced before moving on to heaven. If so, she had nothing to lose. "Go ahead and shoot me," she said. "It won't make any difference."

"Why not?" She heard surprise in his voice and suddenly the metal was no longer near her cheek.

"I'm probably already dead." She turned around and looked into those fierce gray eyes.

"You don't look like a dead woman, Lizzie. Although, in your line of work, I hear women die before their time."

"I'm not a prostitute."

"You're no virgin, either," he stated. "I'd bet my last silver dollar on that fact."

Elizabeth refused to discuss her sex life with an outlaw. "You were going to leave me with that horrible man."

"I paid him well. He was told to leave you alone."

She raised her eyebrows. "And you believed him?"

Logan shrugged. "He gave his word."

"Sure he did." Elizabeth shuddered, remembering the eager look in the man's beady eyes. "He looks like a real gentleman."

"Move over," he said, and waited for her to scoot out of the way before he climbed onto the seat and took the rifle. He opened it and closed it. "It's not loaded. I'd forgotten Billy bought these."

"I'm not going back to that cabin."

He picked up the reins. "As I see it, you don't have a choice."

She thought quickly. She had to have something to bargain with, something that gave her an edge. "There's a price on your head, Mr. Younger. And you're meeting your outlaw gang at Devil's Slide and getting ready to rob another train." The train robbery part was just a guess, but from the way his lips tightened, she knew she'd struck pay dirt. "Your friend Parker, gentleman that he is, would probably appreciate that information, especially if he knew there was a reward. The second you leave me at that horrible cabin, I'm going to make a deal with that little creep and we're going to follow you and bring you back to Salt Lake and split the reward money. I can go back to Boston with seventy-five hundred dollars."

She waited for his response. When he finally spoke, he sounded aggravated. "What's to stop me from killing you right here and now?"

"Shoot a woman in cold blood? You've had plenty of chances today and you haven't done it. I don't think you're going to kill me now."

Logan slapped the reins across the horses' rumps. "Don't tempt me, sweetheart. We're going back to Parker's and you're going to sit in the wagon and keep your mouth shut and your hands off my rifle while I buy an extra horse. Is that clear?"

"I guess so."

Logan completed his business with the disappointed man, tied the spare horse to the wagon, then headed the wagon down the hill and back to the road. Pete Parker knew horseflesh, but he couldn't shoot a squirrel at five feet. And the woman couldn't even tell whether or not a rifle was loaded. They wouldn't be much of a match for him if they decided to track him down. They'd be dead and he'd be on his way to steal another pile of money from the Southern Pacific and hopefully give Crocker and his partners apoplexy.

But he didn't want to kill anyone. He was tired. He'd never shot anyone who hadn't pulled a gun on him first, but people wanted to believe what they wanted to believe, no matter what the truth was. And the truth, well, the truth didn't need repeating when no one believed it in the first place.

Leaving the woman with Parker had been one of his better ideas. The man would have kept her out of the way until long after Logan was gone from the Territory. What happened to her after that was no business of his.

But he couldn't help the nagging feeling that maybe it was. What if she wasn't in cahoots with Al Richardson, after all? She didn't act like a whore. She didn't look like one, either. He couldn't hurt an innocent woman.

Especially an innocent woman with eyes the color of Sarah's.

He couldn't leave her, not as long as she was willing to blab that Logan Younger was around and looking to rob another train. She could recognize him and she could recognize Billy, too.

"Okay," he said as he guided the horses along the trail north. "I'll take you with me."

"Can you take me to a train station?"

"I'll do better than that, sweetheart." He chuckled. He'd forgotten the simple pleasure of driving with a woman in a wagon. "I'll take you right to the train."

THEY TRAVELED until sunset. The pass cut through the base of the Wasatch Mountains, but Logan turned the wagon north as soon as there was a trail to follow. He seemed to know where he was going. Isolated and growing dark, the area gave Elizabeth the chills. It looked like every western movie she'd ever seen. This was outlaw country, and the outlaw with her knew the way through the darkening mountains.

"We'll have to stop." He frowned at the horses. "We'd be faster on horseback, but there's no other way." He waited until he heard water, then guided the horses off the trail and into a small clearing, then stopped the team. "You're not going to pull a gun on me, are you?"

"Not here," she said. It wouldn't be easy to find her way back now. She guessed they were somewhere northeast of Salt Lake, in the mountains she'd admired from her hotel window. She didn't want to be on her own. Not yet. Besides, she was so tired, she wouldn't be able to get far without giving out.

"Your word," he demanded, but there was an amused gleam in his eyes.

"Cross my heart."

"Good enough." He nodded. "Get down and get a fire going. I'll get some water and take care of the horses."

"I don't know how to build a fire." She hopped out of the wagon and stretched. Her bones ached from the hours of being jolted from side to side and her stomach growled. At this rate, she'd be rid of that ten pounds she'd wanted to lose before the wedding. She'd wanted sophisticated cheekbones in her wedding photographs.

"Well, gather some wood, then. Don't wander too far away."

Elizabeth eyed the dark woods. She'd give a lot for a flashlight right now. "Are there dangerous animals in there?"

"Yeah. Two or three hundred, at least." He sounded tired. "Just go to the edge of the clearing and pick up kindling and dry pieces of wood. Bring 'em back here and I'll do the rest."

Still she hesitated. Then, mustering her courage, she gathered her long skirts and took a few steps toward the dark stand of trees. She relieved herself behind some brush, then looked around for wood. It didn't take long to pick up an armload of sticks and twigs, and she hurried back to the wagon where Logan stood. "Is this enough?"

"It's a start," he conceded. "Set it down. I want to see what's in this wagon before dark."

She dumped the armload of wood a few feet away, then brushed the dirt and leaves from the bodice of her dress. She'd taken off her bonnet when the sun lowered, and her hair hung loose and uncombed. She made an effort to comb through the snarls with her fingers, then pushed it away from her face in frustration. The cooling night air smelled fresh and clean, and somewhere above, a bird called. She'd never been camping before. She'd wanted to be a Girl Scout, but it had never happened. One of her foster mothers had enrolled her, but Elizabeth had been moved before the first meeting. After that, she'd realized that she wasn't going to be like the other girls, no matter how much she wanted to be.

"You'll need this," Logan said, stepping up behind her and putting the shawl around her shoulders. He touched her briefly, then backed off as if she were dangerous.

"Thank you." She gathered the fabric to her bodice and turned to smile at him. She hadn't expected to be taken care of.

His expression couldn't be seen in the encroaching darkness, but his voice was gruff. "I'll build that fire now."

She watched as he gathered the smaller sticks and arranged them in a triangular pile. He laid larger sticks above, then pulled matches from a tin holder in his shirt pocket and lit the pile. Tiny flames grew into larger ones, and Logan sat on his haunches and nursed the small fire into a roaring blaze. He set up a metal frame over the campfire and hung a pot on a hook above the flames.

"I could sure use some coffee," he said. He tossed her a blanket. "I guess it's too much to hope that you can cook."

"Nope," she replied cheerfully, making a cushion from the blanket before she sat down. She felt safe now. The fire would scare off wild animals and Logan was going to make something to eat. She'd survived her first day in this strange place, which was no small achievement, considering how many times she'd had a gun pointed at her. She wasn't dead, or at least she didn't think so. As long as she was alive, she had a chance to get back to her life. And to John and their wedding.

She swallowed the sudden lump in her throat. She'd been so close to getting what she'd always wanted. He would be worrying about her. Her plane would have landed and she wouldn't be on it. Would he call the police right away or would he try to track her down in Utah? What would the hotel do with her things when they found out she'd disappeared? Hundreds of people disappeared every year. And some of their stories appeared on television, on "Greatest Unsolved Mysteries." She didn't want to be a fifteen-minute television segment.

"You want coffee?" he asked.

"Please." She looked toward the fire and the steaming pot. Logan threw a handful of ground coffee into the water and, wearing leather gloves, put the lid on. Nothing had ever smelled so good. That is, until he took a knife and cut thick pieces of bacon for a cast-iron skillet that he set above the coals. Her mouth watered as the bacon started to sizzle.

"Guess you haven't traveled much," he said.

"Not like this, no." She shifted on the blanket, trying to get more comfortable. "How long before we get to a train?"

"I'm not sure."

"Tomorrow?"

"Not a chance." He poked at the bacon, moving it around the skillet with his knife. "You in a hurry?"

"A big hurry."

He gazed at her from across the fire. His hat was tipped back and his shirtsleeves rolled up to reveal powerful forearms. This was a man who could take care of himself. "You running away from something?"

"Not exactly. I'm just trying to get home."

"With a share of the bounty money, of course." He broke six eggs into the skillet with the crisping bacon.

"That wasn't my plan, but I'll do whatever it takes to get on a train."

His smile was wry. "I believe you've said that before." He picked up a tin plate and filled it, then tossed a couple of biscuits on top of the bacon. He leaned away from the flames and handed her the plate and a fork, then ladled coffee into tin cups. He set her cup within arm's reach and fixed his own plate. "Eat up," he said. "Tomorrow's going to be another long day."

She picked up the biscuit and broke it apart with her fingers, then copied Logan as he dipped a chunk of biscuit in the grease. A hundred fat grams sure tasted good, especially after hardly eating all day. She ate hungrily, then washed it down with the steaming coffee. It didn't really taste like coffee, but she didn't care.

"You want another biscuit?" Logan offered, tossing another handful into the skillet.

Elizabeth nodded, ravenous.

She almost liked him.

"COME ON."

Something hard nudged her foot. Elizabeth snuggled deeper into her blanket and groaned.

"It's almost daylight," the voice persisted. "You want me to leave you here for the bears to find?"

She kept her eyes closed. A tiny part of her had hoped she'd awaken in her own bed. Or any bed, as long as it was in 1996. "What year is it?"

He sighed. "Do you ask that question every morning?"

"Yes." Elizabeth opened her eyes and tilted her head to see Logan leaning over her, his hands on his hips. He was fully dressed and looked as if he'd been awake for hours.

"It's the same year it was yesterday."

Her heart sank. "I should have known."

"Let's go. There's coffee left, and eggs, too. You'd better hurry if you want to eat."

She'd wrapped the blanket around her and tucked the pillow under her head. She hadn't thought she'd be comfortable, but she'd slept a heavy, dreamless sleep and felt refreshed. Elizabeth hurried off to the bushes, then returned to wash up with water from the creek. She wiped her face on the hem of her dress, then gulped down breakfast while Logan packed up the wagon and hooked up the horses. Eating an apple served as a toothbrush, then she patted the horses' soft noses and said good morning, but Logan had no time to waste. Once she'd climbed onto the wagon seat, he joined her and moved the horses out of the clearing and onto the trail north. The sun hadn't risen over the mountains yet, but the sky was growing lighter by the minute.

Elizabeth adjusted her pillow underneath her, pulled the shawl around her shoulders and watched the Utah morning begin.

LOGAN LIFTED his revolver in the air and fired two shots in succession up into the air before branching off into the narrow canyon. Answering shots rang over the hills, so he knew all was well. Another half an hour and he'd be out of this damn wagon. It had been another long day, but the woman hadn't made any trouble. She did as she was told, didn't gripe about the cold food or the hot sun or anything else, for that matter. He wondered if she was feeling all right. The last thing he needed on his hands was a sick woman, and he already worried about her being crazy.

But she gave him no cause for worry over the many hours they spent on the trail. Now, if she kept her mouth shut and stayed out of everyone's way, he might get through the next three days without any trouble.

"Is this Devil's Slide?" she asked.

"You don't need to know where we are." The horses sped up, as if sensing their journey was almost over. The canyon opened up to a large clearing, where a rough cabin was tucked into the mountain's eastern slope. The wide corral was filled with horses, and smoke curled from the cabin's chimney. Logan's mouth watered. The food would be good tonight.

"Halloo!" a voice called from above them.

Logan waved, relief flooding through him at the sight of Billy perched on the ledge above, a rifle cradled in his hand.

Once they crossed the meadow and approached the cabin, men spilled from the open door to greet them. Their mouths fell open when they saw the woman. He felt her stiffen beside him. "They won't hurt you," he said. "Just keep close to me and don't give anyone cause to think you're available."

She gulped. "I won't."

"Hey, Younger!" A large-bellied, bearded man approached the wagon and grinned. "You made it! Heard you had some trouble. Told you not to go near the city."

Logan hopped down and shook the man's hand. "Yeah, Bob. I should have listened to you."

The man looked over at Elizabeth, then back to Logan. He lowered his voice. "Did you find out where he is?"

"Yeah." He smiled at his friend. "I wired to let him know I was coming soon."

Bob grinned and slapped him on the back. "Good! Good!"

Logan turned to Lizzie, who waited on the wagon seat. "Come on down, Lizzie," he said, lifting his hand to help her. He would treat her like a lady and hope it would set an example for the others. "Bob, this is Lizzie Richards." He deliberately shortened her name so there would be no questions about its similarity to the bounty hunter's name. "She's going to be with us for a few days before she returns to Boston."

Bob nodded politely, but he was clearly shocked. "Boston?"

"Yes. I'm, uh, just visiting," she said.

The other four men hesitated on the porch. Despite Lizzie's scruffy bonnet and oversize dress, she was still obviously a beautiful woman and her appearance in the isolated valley hideout was nothing short of a miracle. Logan took Lizzie's elbow and led her toward the cabin.

There was a sense of finality to this, Logan realized. This would be his last trip to the Slide and he wouldn't shed tears over leaving this place behind. A few more days and the nightmare would be over.

LOGAN SENT HER inside the one-room cabin after dinner, while he and the others gathered on the porch to smoke and drink and plan whatever they were planning. He was obviously their leader, she decided. It was easy to see. Billy, though older, hung on Logan's every word and clearly looked upon him as a son. Bob, the large bearded man, was about Logan's age, and in charge of the cooking and the cabin. There were four others, young towheaded men who eyed her shyly and

kept their distance. They were the Cramer brothers,
Logan had explained. He didn't say what their first
names were.

Logan had shown her how to light a kerosene lamp
and she'd found her way to the outhouse. He'd brought
her a basin of warm water and a rough bar of lye soap.
She would wash herself as best she could while the
outlaws had their meeting and smoked their cigars.

She planned to listen to their conversation carefully
and learn what was going to happen, so that she would
be prepared for anything, but the low hum of male
voices put her to sleep minutes after she lay down on
her makeshift pallet in the corner of the cabin. She
didn't waken until a man sat down next to her on the
floor. She held her breath and waited in the darkness.
A man was snoring out on the porch and an owl hooted
nearby. "Logan?" she whispered. There was little
moonlight and the cabin was black.

"Yeah," he answered. "I thought you were asleep."

"I was."

She heard his boots thump on the floor, then the
rustle of blankets. "What are you doing?"

"Getting some rest. I hope."

"Here?"

"I thought it would be best," he said, sighing as he
stretched out beside her. "Considering you're the only
woman here and I'm the one who brought you."

"Oh." She lay back down and listened to his even
breathing. She should have realized how vulnerable she
still was, might always be, in this untamed land. Salt
Lake had been civilized, with attractive buildings and
neat streets, but she was far from the city now. And
Logan was very close. She could reach out and touch
his face easily enough, but she didn't try. She didn't

want to touch him. She didn't want him this close to her. Last night, he'd slept on the other side of the fire and seemed miles away. This was different. If she turned her head, she could feel his breath. She waited for long moments, wondering what he would do next. Finally, realizing she was safe, she dared to close her eyes.

He listened to the sound of her breathing and waited for her to relax. He hadn't been able to resist sleeping beside her. It had been such a long time since he'd slept beside a woman, her hair a neat braid draped over one breast, her hips swaying under her nightgown.

Lizzie was in no danger as long as she was with him. These men would do her no harm. They were farmers, not cold-blooded killers. They'd been robbed of much more than their land, but they hadn't turned mean.

He lay awake for a long time, listening to her breathe. He heard when her breathing became deep and rhythmic and knew she'd fallen back to sleep. He relaxed then, and stayed awake as long as he could so he could enjoy having a woman sleeping beside him.

In the morning, just before dawn lightened the sky to charcoal gray, Logan awoke. The woman was curled against him. Her cheek rested on his upper arm and her hand lay spread on his chest. She'd sought his warmth in the night, as Sarah used to. In the morning, finding her against him, he would slip his hand under her gown and stroke her warm skin until she awoke and smiled her consent to early-morning loving.

He grew hard remembering the soft feel of being inside a willing woman at dawn. He looked down at Lizzie, sleeping so sweetly against his aching body. She was a delicate-looking little thing, with a stubborn streak that rivaled his own. She would not be passive in his arms, and she hadn't argued when he'd said she was no virgin. He could take her, he knew. He could take her and not a man here would stop him. Hell, they already thought he'd had her.

Careful not to wake her, Logan took his free hand and touched one finger to her face, drawing a line across her flushed cheek to her lips. With a muffled groan, he dropped his hand and eased himself away from her. He wasn't a man who took a woman against her will, no matter how long it had been since he'd taken his pleasure with one. He pulled on his boots and stumbled outside, taking great gulps of air as he fled the cabin.

"OL' JESSE JAMES DIED about four years ago," Billy explained, leaning closer to the fire. "Killed by one of his own gang, the story goes. Shot in the back by his best friend while he was standin' on a chair hangin' a picture."

"Really?" Lizzie hung on to every word.

"Yep."

"Did you know him?"

"No, ma'am. But everyone heard of him, if you know what I mean." He turned to Logan. "You knew him, didn't you?"

"My uncles did." He didn't look happy about admitting it.

"Were they outlaws, too?" Lizzie asked.

Billy coughed, choking on his coffee.

Logan frowned at him, then looked into the fire. "You've never heard of the Younger brothers, Lizzie?"

"No, I don't think so." She tried to remember what the book had said. "They're in my book. I'll go get it."

"Your uncles still alive?" one of the Cramer brothers asked Logan. "Were they as tough as everyone said?"

"Yeah. Bob, Cole and Jim are in prison," Logan answered, and Lizzie slipped away from the campfire to retrieve her book from Logan's saddlebag. He'd stored his things in the corner of the cabin where they'd slept last night. She found it easily, tucked above a thick wad of hundred-dollar bills. The lantern above the stove provided enough light to see that there was a small fortune in the saddlebag.

No wonder he'd been disturbed by her arrival in his hotel room. He was an outlaw, a man who had stolen thick wads of money from trains or banks. He had a lot to lose, and the life of one woman wouldn't figure in his plans. She replaced the money and took her book, then refastened the buckle that held the flap of the bag closed.

When she rejoined the men around the campfire, they stopped talking. She took her place on the log between Bob and Logan and set the book on her knees.

"What kind of a book is that, ma'am?" Billy leaned around Logan to peer at the cover. "It's real pretty, but it looks kinda beat-up."

"I think it must be very old. It's called *Rogues Across Time* and it's about famous men in history. There's a section on outlaws and gunslingers," she announced. "I thought there might be something on your, uh, relatives." She opened the book and flipped through the pages until she found what she was looking for. The odd feeling of light-headedness skimmed through her again as she saw the sketch of Logan's face on the wanted poster. "It's you, but it doesn't give your name."

He frowned and took a closer look, tilting the book toward the light of the campfire. "Could be anybody. I'm not that famous, not enough to be in a book."

Bob leaned over to study the page. "Definitely a Younger, though. Look at the chin. The eyes, too."

"What does it say? Will you read it to us?" Billy urged. The blond brothers nodded.

Elizabeth looked at Logan, who nodded his reluctant approval. "Go ahead," he said. "I guess it can't hurt."

She read the description of the outlaws, omitting any action that happened after 1886. She didn't tell them that Frank James eventually joined Buffalo Bill's Wild West Show or that an affable outlaw called Butch Cassidy would team up with the Sundance Kid in about ten years and terrorize this part of the country.

Bob peered over her shoulder. "What else is in that book?"

She flipped to the table of contents. "Pirates, Indians, Vikings—"

"Read about the pirates," Billy interrupted. "My father used to tell me stories about pirates."

"All right." She read that page and others, and turned the book to show the sketches as if she were reading to a group of children. The rough group of men showed great delight in discussing the merits of each kind of adventurer after Elizabeth's throat became dry and she began to lose her voice. Bob handed her a cup and she took a swallow, thinking it was coffee. Whiskey burned her throat and she choked.

Logan took the cup from her fingers and with his free hand hit her on the back. "Whoa, there," he said, then bit back a smile. "Guess you can't hold your liquor."

"I wasn't expecting it," she said, retrieving the cup and draining it. She wasn't normally a drinker, but falling into another century and hanging out with an outlaw gang was turning her into someone different.

Her stomach warmed and she felt better. She'd felt unsettled since handling the book. It was time to put it away. If there were certain powers attached to it, then she wanted to save them until she was back in that Salt Lake hotel room.

"Time to turn in," Logan said, standing up. The rest of the men followed. Logan automatically gave her his hand and helped her step over the log, and dropped it as soon as she was steady on her feet. The minute he touched her, a steady feeling of peace flooded her body. She'd never felt anything like it before.

She walked beside him to the cabin and took her place on the makeshift bed on the floor. He turned off the kerosene lamp, then sat down with his back to her and pulled off his boots. She shoved the book under her pillow, settled herself on the blanket and pulled the shawl around her shoulders.

"You've got yourself quite a book," he said, stretching out beside her. "It sure entertained the boys tonight."

"Was that really you in the picture?"

"Might be, might not. Doesn't make any difference, anyway."

"I guess not," she agreed, but she wished she understood why the book and that particular page, the one with Logan's picture, had drawn her from her safe, secure life into an uncertain future with a band of outlaws. There was a connection, but she didn't want to be connected any longer. She wanted to go home. "When are you taking me to the train?"

"Soon," he promised. "Real soon."

"Before you rob the train or after?"

There was a long moment of silence. "During," Logan said finally. "You can climb aboard and tell everyone you were kidnapped by a gang of ruthless outlaws, but by the time the deputy marshals arrive, we'll be long gone. I'll give you enough money to go home."

"Thank you."

"I'd appreciate it if you didn't make our descriptions too accurate, though you're welcome to use my name."

"I saw the money in your bag," she whispered. "Why don't you quit while you're ahead?" She thought of Frank James. "Some outlaws retire, don't they, before they let themselves get killed?"

"I can't quit. Not yet."

She thought about that for a minute. "Why do you do this?"

He sighed, a heavy sound in the quiet night. "Lady, the railroad didn't give me much choice."

"What do you mean?" She moved onto her side, wanting to hear how a good man turned bad.

"You're asking too many questions. Go to sleep. We're through telling stories tonight."

She heard the rustle of his blankets and knew he'd turned away from her. Logan Younger had a bagful of money and plans to rob another train. He was an outlaw. She should be terrified, she told herself. Instead, she knew that nothing bad would happen to her as long as Logan was around.

4

THEY HIT the trail two days later, early in the morning.
The men stored their possessions in fat bedrolls behind
their saddles, and Elizabeth learned from Billy that
Bob, the cheerful bearded man who did all the cooking, was the only man planning to return to the Devil's
Slide cabin. Despite the man's protests, Logan assigned the youngest of the brothers the job of staying
at the cabin and taking care of the spare horses until
Bob returned. He was told where to meet his brothers
in two weeks.

Elizabeth perched atop a plain brown gelding. He
seemed content to follow the other horses along the trail
without any extra instruction from her. No one asked
her if she could ride. Logan had given her a pair of pants
and a dirty flannel shirt to wear, then packed the rest
of her meager belongings into a small roll. One of the
blond brothers, claiming he'd bought a new one, had
tossed her a soft, dented cowboy hat. Then Logan
tossed her into the saddle, adjusted the stirrups for her
feet and told her to keep up.

She held the reins in one hand, the way Logan did.
And she gripped the pommel of the saddle, the way
Logan didn't. It was there, she decided, noting the
amused looks from Billy, so she may as well make the
most of the help.

They traveled for hours, until her rear end ached and her thighs cramped. The sun was high when Logan stopped to water the horses.

"You getting down?" he said, pausing beside her horse. "You've got to eat."

Elizabeth tried to swing her right leg over the saddle, but her muscles protested. "I can't," she admitted. "I'm not much of a rider."

"Here," he said, reaching for her. His large hands fit around her waist and he lifted her easily from the saddle and steadied her on her feet. When he attempted to release her, she toppled forward and he was forced to hold her to his chest until her knees stopped trembling.

She fought the urge to wrap her arms around him, instead stepping out of his arms as soon as her legs would hold her. "Sorry," she said, feeling foolish.

He tipped his hat. "No problem," he said, and reached for her horse. Elizabeth stepped away as Logan led the animal to the sandy creek.

She walked gingerly over to where Bob was passing out rations of bread and salted beef. He grinned at her. "Not used to ridin', I see."

She took the food and sat down on the grass beside him. "Now I know why cowboys are bowlegged."

"It ain't an easy life," he agreed, handing her a canteen. "Drink up. It's gonna be a long day, if Younger has anything to say about it."

"Are you robbing the train today?"

He shook his head. "No, we've got days of ridin' to do yet."

"Do you know where we are?"

"I know where we're headin', that's all that matters."

"Where?"

"To rob the Southern Pacific." He leaned back against the tree trunk. "In order to do that, we're headin' west."

"Aren't there any trains closer?"

"Sure. Wouldn't be the same," he said, chewing another mouthful of bread. "Gotta be the Southern Pacific. Runs north to south in California and east from Sacramento to Ogden."

"Why?"

He shrugged. "Just the way it is."

"No, I mean why do you have to rob the Southern Pacific trains?"

Bob smiled, but it was a smile that made her blood run cold. "Good reasons," he said.

"Oh." She bit into the bread and decided she should try to change the subject. "You're a good cook. Were you a cook before you became an outlaw?"

Bob laughed, making his big belly shake. "No, ma'am. I never considered myself a cook *or* an outlaw." He chuckled again. "I'm a simple farmer." He swung his arm to include the band of men lounging under the shade of the trees eating their noon meal. "We're all simple farmers."

"Even Logan?"

"Yeah," he nodded. "Logan, too."

"When did you all stop farming?"

He gave her a sharp look. "He didn't tell you?"

She knew who "he" was. "No," she admitted, taking another bit of bread and washing it down with water that tasted like metal. "He's not much for conversation."

"Well," Bob drawled, watching the tall outlaw check a horse's hoof. "Life ain't easy." He paused, choosing his words carefully. "And there's those who don't like to talk about the hard times."

They sat in companionable silence and ate their meal. Logan approached them and ate his share of the food standing up nearby. When he was done, he gave the signal and the men moved to their horses. Bob helped Elizabeth to her feet.

"He's going to torture me until I reach that train," she muttered, willing her legs to hold her upright.

"Logan's a different man since Sarah died." Bob patted her on the back as Logan turned to frown at them.

"Come on," he yelled. "We don't have all day!"

"Who is Sarah?"

Bob looked surprised. "His wife."

"Logan was *married?*" She didn't know why that surprised her. He was a handsome man. Surely any number of women would be happy to be with him, despite his risky life-style. She didn't think of him as the domestic type, couldn't visualize him sharing the cooking duties or washing dishes.

"Yeah." Bob gave her an odd look. "Sarah was a right nice girl, too. She—"

"Shut up," Logan snapped. He glared at the older man and motioned for him to move away from Elizabeth. "Don't mention her name," he growled. "Not here, not now."

Bob eyed the outlaw with sympathy. "My apologies, Logan. It won't happen again."

Elizabeth stood stunned at the ravaged expression in Logan's gray eyes. She'd seen that look before, when she was a child. She'd seen it on the new kid's face when he realized he'd been torn from his family. She'd seen it in a worker's eyes when she'd looked at a battered child she'd rescued from his parents. Oh, she'd seen that expression before, all right. Pain that came right from the heart. "I'm sorry," she whispered, hating to see someone suffer like that.

"Get on your horse," he told her, his hands on his hips.

"I don't know why you're so angry," she said, turning her back to him as she headed for her horse. He was handsome, in a tough, scruffy way, she mused. He hadn't shaved for days, though he was clean-shaven when she met him five days ago. It was now Tuesday, she realized. John would be frantic, of course. The police would be involved and no trace of her would have been found. "It's stupid of me to feel sorry for you."

"It's none of your damn business," he said, following her. "I didn't ask for this."

She spun around on her heels. "And neither did I. I didn't ask to be kidnapped and dragged over mountains, I didn't want to be here and I don't know how to get back—" Angry, she blinked back tears and tried to mount her horse. She was so damn tired of being bossed around.

He took her by the waist and turned her around, then bent his head to hers. Their lips met in an angry embrace that knocked the breath back in her throat. His whiskers burned her skin, but his lips were hard as he slanted them across her mouth. It was a harsh kiss, a kiss that made no sense and yet she knew it was inevitable. His fingers tightened on her waist, but he didn't pull her against him. A tiny corner of her heart recognized there was nothing to fear, yet she pushed at his chest with her palms. It was like pushing on an iron door.

"Get on the goddam horse," he said, looking down at her with glittering eyes. "And try to keep up."

"Take your hands off me," she said, trapped between Logan and the patient horse.

He removed his hands from her waist and took a step back. He tipped his hat in a mocking gesture and waited for her to mount the animal without help. Elizabeth struggled to reach the stirrup, but the brown gelding kept shying away. She swore under her breath as Logan touched her again. He lifted her into the saddle and walked away without a word.

Elizabeth picked up the reins and waited for Logan to mount up. Her skin burned where his whiskers had rubbed; she could still feel his fingers at her waist. She'd never been kissed like that, never felt such angry need in a man's embrace. He'd hated the fact that he wanted her. She could tell by the expression on his face.

She prayed he'd stay away.

THAT NIGHT she took the book from her bedroll and held it tightly against her chest as she lay under her blanket at the edge of the campfire. Logan lay close to her, as usual, his large body angled near hers. He hadn't made a move toward her since noon. He had avoided her, had assigned Billy to watch over her when she made her nightly trip into the brush.

It had been a long day, Logan leading them north, through an isolated area of the mountains where they saw no one else. If there were towns, he was avoiding them. If there were homesteads, he was keeping out of sight. Her muscles ached from the long hours in the saddle. She would have given half her life for a hot bath, a hairbrush and a roll of toilet paper.

She wanted to go home. Like the little girl in *The Wizard of Oz*, she wanted to click her heels together and go back to Kansas. Elizabeth wrapped her arms around the book and waited for something, anything, to happen. She'd slept with it once before and landed in another century. Why couldn't that happen again? She should have thought of trying this before. Maybe she didn't have to be in that room, in that hotel, in that city for the magic to work.

She closed her eyes and imagined walking through the Lovell mansion, past the hand-knotted Oriental rugs and the Duncan Phyfe furniture. She pretended she was married and resting in the wide bed with the carved pineapples on the four posters. The lace coverlet was a wedding present from John's grandmother, the goose-feather pillows a shower gift from her staff at work.

Tonight she would sleep and when she awoke, the man beside her under smooth cotton sheets would be John. He would smile when she brought his coffee. He would tell her he didn't know what he would do without her and she would agree that she didn't know, either.

"TIME TO MOVE," Logan growled. He placed a tin cup near her. "Coffee," he snapped. "Drink up and do what you have to do. We're out of here in ten minutes."

Elizabeth struggled to sit up, and the book dropped to the ground. She picked it up and rubbed the worn cover. It was cold and stiff, nothing more than an old book. That solved that. She was still in 1886. Going to bed with the book was not the answer. There was some other combination that was needed to unlock the future. The hotel room, she decided. That would be her next try. She wouldn't have long to wait, just a few more days. She tossed the book aside and reached for the coffee. The men made quick motions of packing up and getting ready to ride. She would have to hurry or Logan would return, and from experience, she knew he wasn't exactly a morning person.

THEY TOOK a long break at noon. Several of the men stretched out under trees, their hats covering their faces while they napped. It didn't take Logan long to realize that Billy and Elizabeth were missing. He heard their voices and followed the sound past a stand of trees to the edge of another clearing. Billy was holding a revolver, while Elizabeth stood close beside him.

Logan strode forward into sight. "What in hell are you doing?"

Billy placed the Colt .45 in Elizabeth's hand as Logan stepped closer. "Teaching the lady how to handle a gun."

"Why on earth would you do that?"

He shrugged. "She oughta know how to protect herself."

"She's protected," he snapped. "There are six men here who never let her out of their sight." He took the revolver from her palm. "Give me that," he said sharply. "You'll kill one of us for sure."

"Learning how to defend myself is not a bad idea," she protested, looking longingly at the gun. "What if we're attacked by Indians?"

Logan checked the barrel to make certain it was empty. "You've been reading too many dime novels." He turned to Billy. "You're to keep her away from guns from now on, unless I tell you different."

"Geez, Logan. We were just havin' fun."

"Yeah, and last week this *lady* shows up in my hotel room claiming to know there's a price on my head. Have you forgotten that?"

"Sorry, ma'am. Guess this wasn't such a good idea, after all."

"I'm not going to hurt anyone," Elizabeth said. Billy shot her an apologetic look and crossed the clearing.

Logan looked down at the gun, then back at her. "You going to shoot me with this?"

She lifted her chin, an act of defiance that was spoiled by the tinge of red on the side of her lips where his whiskers had burned her skin. "Not unless you touch me again."

He ignored her warning and placed one finger on her cheek. "I did this to you? My apologies. I'd forgotten there are good reasons to shave." He dropped his hand and fingered the revolver, instead. "You planning to kill someone?"

Her eyes grew wide. "No."

"Wrong answer. When you carry a gun, you have to figure you're going to use it."

"I thought I could protect myself, especially if you're determined to rob a train."

He sighed. "You'll get us all killed, Lizzie. And maybe yourself, too. If you have a gun, you could be mistaken for an outlaw and get hurt." The thought made his stomach roll sickeningly. He shut his eyes briefly, trying to blot out the image of blood staining a pink-flowered dress as Sarah lay slumped in the middle of the wheat field.

"Just show me how to use it," Elizabeth begged. "I don't want to carry a gun, but it seems like a woman out here in the West ought to know how to protect herself. For her own safety."

"You're safe enough." From a distance, she looked like a boy with her hair tucked underneath that old hat. The pants were baggy, the collarless shirt buttoned high to her neck. The outline of her high breasts and the curve of her hips pointed out that she was a woman, though. Any fool could see that. If anything happened to him, the others had instructions to see that she got on the train. But anything could go wrong. She could be left behind, at the mercy of any man who came along.

Whoever or whatever she was, she didn't deserve that.

He held out the revolver. "It's been called a peace-maker," he said gruffly. "Take it and see if you can hold it straight."

THEY CAMPED by a sandy stream that evening, long before the sun disappeared over the distant horizon. Logan hadn't pushed as hard in the last hours, so Elizabeth had the impression that they were making good time and he was satisfied with their progress.

Elizabeth leaned over the shallow water and splashed her heated skin. She unbuttoned her shirt as much as she dared, then drizzled water between her breasts. The water was warm, heated all day by the sun. It was tempting to throw herself into the stream the way the men had, uncaring of their clothes and filling their hats with water to rinse their heads. They'd left boots and guns and holsters and rifles along the bank after they'd watered the horses.

She'd learned that horses always came first, and after two days in the saddle, she understood why.

Logan waded out of the water. His wide chest was covered with dark curling hair. He didn't seem to mind that she was staring at him. He'd removed his shirt and rinsed it, and was now squeezing excess water from the dripping fabric. "You need a bath, too, Lizzie."

"Not with an audience."

"Fair enough." He nodded and hung his shirt over a bush to dry. After the last man had staggered from the creek, picked up his possessions and headed for camp, Logan waved a hand toward the water. "It's all yours."

He must think she was stupid. She was not going to remove her clothes and, stark naked, throw herself into the water while he was standing there. "After you leave."

He grinned, and she realized he was teasing. He pulled on his boots, then lifted his shirt from the bush and put it on, not bothering to button it closed. "Just holler if you need help."

"Uh, Logan?"

"Yeah?"

"Can I borrow your soap?"

He rummaged through his belongings and pulled out a bar of soap, then tossed it to her. She caught it neatly. "Thanks."

"Take your time," he said, watching her hurry to untie her boots. "The creek's not going anywhere."

She waited for him to scramble over the sandy bank and disappear out of sight before she unbuttoned the rest of her shirt. She looked around cautiously, feeling strange. She'd never removed her clothes outdoors before and she couldn't escape the feeling that it wasn't safe. She waited a long minute more, while birds chirped in the trees on the opposite bank and a sage-scented breeze cooled her skin. She was alone for the first time in days.

She picked up the soap and, still clothed, waded tentatively into the water until she was chest-deep. Ducking to her shoulders, she removed her clothes under the cover of the water, then rubbed the soap over her skin.

She eyed the creek bank, but no one appeared to gawk at her, so she ducked her head and scrubbed her hair until she was satisfied that five days of Utah dust was gone.

Much later, after she'd put on her shirt and climbed out of the water, she sat on the edge of the water and waited for her clothes to dry. Although the shirt hung to her knees, she couldn't walk past the men with her legs exposed. The year 1886 wasn't ready for such scandalous behavior.

Logan would kill her.

She heard footsteps above her and knew Logan had come. "What the hell is taking you so long?" he called.

She turned around to look up at him and hugged her knees to her chest, trying to discreetly cover herself. "I'm waiting for my clothes to dry."

"Here." Logan tossed her blue dress down to her. "Put this on and get back to camp."

She caught it in midair, before it could land in the dirt. "Thanks." She heard his footsteps move away, then removed her damp shirt and pulled the dress over her head. It was so big that she did up the back hooks, twisted the dress around to the back, then slipped her arms into the sleeves. He hadn't brought the under-clothing, but she could do without them for now. The baggy blue dress wasn't going to inspire anyone to lust. In fact, the men treated her more like a sister than anything else, but she supposed Logan was responsible for that. And now that he'd taught her the basics of handling a gun, she felt a little safer. At least she could defend herself, if it became necessary.

Even Logan had seen the sense behind that.

Elizabeth combed her hair with her fingers, then pulled it back into a ponytail with a leather strip she'd found at the cabin.

Deciding to leave her pants and shirt to dry, she picked up her boots and hat and climbed barefoot up the bank to the camp. Logan stood waiting, his back to her. He'd probably stood there the entire time, she realized. Again, that strange feeling of being protected swept through her. In his own way, the outlaw was taking care of her.

And, in order to survive until she returned to Boston, she would need all the help she could get.

LOGAN HATED wanting her. He hated watching her and wanting to gather all that long soft hair in his fingers and pull her toward him. He hated the fact that her skin was soft and her smile unconsciously brave.

He should never have given her those pants. Because he especially hated the way his body reacted when he saw her seated on a horse.

Now they were sitting around the campfire. It had been a long day, but Elizabeth had never complained, even though he'd had to lift her off the saddle when they'd stopped to make camp.

He sat beside her, as was his place. Some of the men lit cigars, others stared into the flames. Elizabeth appeared deep in thought as she curled up in front of the flames. She smelled of soap, fresh and sweet, and was still wearing the dress. Which helped. Having a woman parading around in pants was damn unsettling.

Billy cleared his throat. "Did you bring that book with you, Miz Elizabeth?"

She looked up. "Yes. Of course."

"Would you, er, mind readin' a little more tonight? I sure wouldn't mind a little education this evenin'."

"I wouldn't mind," she said, starting to rise.

Logan put his arm on hers. "I'll get it," he offered, and moved through the darkness to her bedroll. She'd slept with the book in her arms last night. She'd brought it with her to the hotel room where he'd slept. She seemed to be uncommonly attached to it. He lifted the book and riffled through the pages. There didn't seem to be anything special about it. Just words and pictures, same as all books.

He wondered if Danny had learned to read and write. If not, he would teach him himself, as soon as they got settled. Logan returned to Elizabeth's side and handed her the book.

"What would you like me to read?" she asked. "We've already read about outlaws and pirates."

Bob blew a smoke ring toward the night sky. "You pick."

Billy nodded his agreement and they all waited for her to begin. Logan watched her face, glad of the excuse to look at her. He half listened to the words she read, not really interested in knowledge tonight. At least not the kind that came out of books.

When she finished, the men thanked her politely. Logan could tell they were hoping she'd continue, but he interrupted with a question of his own.

"Is that your book?"

She placed it carefully on her knees as if it was the most valuable thing on earth. "Yes. I just bought it a few days ago, in Salt Lake City."

Logan ignored the curious expressions of his men. It wasn't considered polite *or* safe to ask personal questions of another man, and the courtesy extended to women, too. "You said you were from Boston. Utah Territory is a a long way from Boston. Are you one of them socialites heading for California?"

"No. I'm going back to Boston as soon as I can."

"And when exactly will that be?"

Bob shot Logan a warning look. "I don't think the lady is interested in answering your questions," he said.

Logan shrugged. He was edgy, and he felt like picking a fight. "Maybe not, but I've asked damn few of them that ever got an answer. Anyone have a problem with that?"

Elizabeth picked up her book, stood up and brushed off her skirt with her free hand. "I'm going to bed."

"Good idea," Logan agreed, standing beside her. "Billy, you take the first watch." He waited for someone to protest, but no one did. As if sensing that their boss was looking for trouble, none of them chose to give him what he wanted. Logan followed Elizabeth to their blankets several yards from the fire. He watched as she settled the book under her pillow and lay down on her side, facing away from him, the rough gray blanket pulled over her shoulder.

He sat on his blanket and balanced his rifle on his knees. He double-checked to see that it was loaded and ready for trouble before he set it beside him. The nights had grown colder the farther north they traveled, and he was glad for his long coat. It was old, but the rips had been mended and the material still provided warmth. That was all that mattered.

"How long were you married?" the woman suddenly asked, her voice soft. He could barely hear her. She turned onto her back and looked up at him.

"Bob has a big mouth."

"He said your wife died. I'm sorry."

"Yeah." They were all sorry. Everyone but Crocker and his gang of thieves that ran the Southern Pacific.

"Is that why you became an outlaw or were you one before then?"

"Maybe it's my turn to ask a question," he drawled, eyeing her as she huddled there under the blanket.

"Go ahead."

"Why were you in Salt Lake City? You're no Mormon woman, unless you're running away. Did your husband beat you? Or kick you out?"

"That's three questions."

"Then I'd appreciate three answers."

"I was in town on business. I've never been married, so no man has beaten me or kicked me out of his house. I think I told you once before that I'm going to be married soon, in just a few weeks, so it's very important I return to Boston as soon as possible."

Her voice shook as she spoke of Boston. She would return there, he thought, and become someone's wife. A man who would sit beside her on their bed at night, a man who would have the right to touch her. "You're not telling me the whole truth."

"You wouldn't believe me if I did."

Logan realized she'd said that before. And she was right. There wasn't a whole lot he'd believe that came out of lips in a face so pretty. "Maybe you have a point," he conceded.

"You have to answer my question," she reminded him.

There was a long moment of silence while Logan considered what she'd asked. "I come from a long line of outlaws and gunslingers," he told her. "But no, I didn't become one myself until after my wife died."

"What happened?" she whispered, her gaze on his face. She propped her head on her elbow and waited for his answer.

"That's not something I like to remember," he told her. He lay down beside her, closer than he'd intended, but she didn't shrink away from him.

"I'm sorry," she said once again.

"Go to sleep." He waited for her to lay down again. He heard the sound of her breathing and knew when she fell asleep. She would roll closer to him in the night. She always did. She sought the warmth of his body and the comfort of his arms and he did nothing to prevent her. In the dark, he could pretend she was Sarah.

In the morning, before he opened his eyes, he would imagine his wife snuggled against him and he would grow hard from wanting her. And when he opened his eyes and saw Elizabeth, he still wanted her.

He wanted her with a force that took hours to dispel.

Logan lay in the dark and listened to the night sounds around him. He was bone-weary, but he fought sleep in order to listen to the woman's rhythmic breathing for a few moments more. Tomorrow, she would be gone.

Tomorrow night, he would sleep alone.

"WEAR THE DRESS over your pants," Logan ordered when Elizabeth gathered her clothes together for the day's ride.

"Why?"

"I don't want you mistaken for one of us."

She stared up at him with those blue eyes. "You're robbing the train today?"

He nodded and saw the relief in her eyes. "You'll soon be free," he assured her. "If everything goes as planned."

"What's the plan?"

He handed her a wad of fifty-dollar bills. "This should get you where you need to go," he said. "Just do as you're told and you'll probably live to see Boston again." He moved away, anxious to hurry the boys along. He wanted to be in position by early afternoon, but he didn't want to push the horses too hard.

From now on, it was a matter of luck and timing. He hoped like hell his luck would hold, just for another twenty-four hours. Once they came out of the cover of the mountains and appeared in the open, there was no telling what would happen. He hoped he'd brought enough dynamite.

5

"Now," Logan cried as the train neared a sparse group of trees, the only protection in miles of open land. Elizabeth waited there, close enough to see what was going on and ready to ride when Logan gave the signal. She was to ride to the train after the outlaws rode away. She was to throw her hands in the air and shout, "Help me," so no one would mistake her for a robber and shoot her.

Logan had advised her to act terrified. She wouldn't have to pretend to be afraid, she knew. She was afraid for all of them as the train ground to a screeching halt. She'd seen movies with train robberies and someone inevitably got shot.

The engineers had spotted the obstruction of branches and rocks on the track and Billy's lantern signaling stop. All at once, Logan and the other four men rushed the engine and ordered the engineer to raise his hands and not put up a fight. Once the engineers agreed, Logan trotted the horse down to the mail car.

"Open it up," he ordered.

There was silence from behind the car, then the grinding of the door as it slid open to reveal a frightened young man in a brown suit. "Don't shoot," he begged.

"Thank you," Logan said, dismounting. He gave the reins to one of the boys. "Give me the keys to the safe."

Elizabeth watched the curious passengers press their faces against the windows. She heard a baby wail into the sudden silence as the young man shook his head. "No, sir."

"No matter," Logan said easily. He waved, and Bob jumped off his horse and arranged the dynamite, then motioned to everyone to move out of the way. The young man hopped out of the car. Seconds later, the safe was blasted open in an explosion of flame and smoke, and Elizabeth's horse spooked and shot sideways. She had all she could do to keep him under control of the reins she'd let go lax, but it was too late. Billy rode over to help her, which gave the conductor time to draw a gun and fire.

She heard the shot and felt a searing heat slash across her right arm. She clutched the saddle horn to keep from falling sideways as Billy grabbed the gelding's bridle. He swore at the animal until the horse, blowing through his nostrils, settled down. She heard Logan swearing while a woman on the train screamed.

"Get her out of the way!" he called. Elizabeth looked for him and finally spotted him waving down two of the brothers from the open car. They tossed heavy canvas bags to Logan, who swung them over his saddle. Bob was holding a gun on the white-faced conductor; the other brother had his rifle pointed toward the window of the engine. There were no more shots from anywhere on the train.

Elizabeth ignored the odd numbness in her arm and waited for Logan to gallop away. She was within minutes of being on that train and returning to her own life. She never doubted that she could use the book to slip through time. If it worked once, it could work again. She had to keep thinking that way, or she would surely go insane. So she ignored the burning in her arm and watched and waited, counting the seconds and holding on to the saddle while Billy urged her horse back into the cover of the trees.

"No," she protested. "I have to get on the train."

"Not 'til Logan says," Billy countered, keeping a steel grip on the bridle. He was half leaning off his own horse in order to control hers.

"Leave me," she insisted. "I'm to wait until you've left before I show myself."

"You already showed yourself," he muttered, staying beside her. "It only got you into trouble. And, lady, you've sure got a way of gettin' yourself into trouble."

"Let's go," Logan called, spinning his horse away from the train. His gun stayed pointed at the conductor.

"This is the last time you'll get away with this!" cried the young man in the brown suit. "I know who you are!"

Logan smiled, a grim smile that made the young man shrink back into the safe shadow of the open car. "I hope to hell you do. Tell Crocker I said we're even now."

He turned his horse and galloped toward the grove of trees, with the rest of the men behind him. He looked furious as he neared her and gave her arm an odd look. "I thought I told you to stay out of sight!"

"The explosion," she managed to say. Another fire-like pain slashed up her arm and she swayed in the saddle. She didn't want to lose her balance. She didn't want to think about the pain. She didn't know what was wrong, but she wanted to get on the train before anything else happened. "The train—"

"Damn," someone said. Then a younger voice asked, "Is she shot bad?"

Elizabeth blinked, and looked sideways. Red ran down her arm, staining the blue sleeve with its dark trail. She looked back at Logan and felt the blood drain from her face before everything went black.

Logan caught her as she swayed toward him. She was light in his arms. Blue calico spilled across his saddle as he settled her in front of him. "Take the reins," he snapped, unwilling to leave the horse behind.

"Leave her," Bob said. "They'll take care of her. That train ain't goin' anywhere 'til they clear the track. We've got to get out of here, pronto!"

"No," he said. He couldn't leave her, not in the middle of nowhere with strangers. He didn't have time to think. He had to get out of here. They all did. They might think she was one of the outlaws left behind. It could take them hours to find out she was an innocent victim and by that time she could have bled to death. "If one of us goes back to that train, we'll get shot for sure."

He couldn't—wouldn't—leave her. Ignoring Bob's protests, Logan cradled her unconscious body with his left arm and kicked his horse into a gallop toward the safety of the distant hills.

Once they reached cover, Billy helped get Elizabeth off the horse, and Logan applied a makeshift tourniquet from fabric he tore from the petticoat in Elizabeth's pack. He took a knife and cut her sleeve, then peeled away as much of the bloody material as he could. The bleeding hadn't stopped, but the wound didn't look bad. The bullet had grazed her upper arm, but he couldn't tell if it was any worse than that, he told

Logan. She'd been lucky, he added, if you could call yourself lucky for getting shot.

But she wasn't going to die. At least, not unless infection set in. There was always that chance, but Logan carried a few medical supplies. Anyone who traveled the mountains did.

"I figure we've got about three hours," Bob said. He looked at the sky and back to Logan. He gestured toward the canvas bags. "You want me to do it?"

"Yeah. The other money is in my saddlebags. Just put my share back in there and leave me the extra horse."

Logan cradled Elizabeth in his arms, not knowing if he wanted her to wake up or not. Women were delicate creatures, all right. It might be best if she stayed faint-like for a while longer. That arm was going to hurt, whether you were used to gunshot wounds or not.

Elizabeth moved in his arms. "Damn it," she muttered, opening her eyes and looking up at him. Her face was still paper-white and her blue eyes clouded with pain. "Damn it all to hell."

"Don't cuss at me," he told her, not bothering to hide his smile. It was a relief to hear her voice, no matter what she was saying. At least he knew she was still alive. He'd had his doubts there for a few minutes. "I'm not the one who shot you."

"Who did?"

"None of us, I can assure you. The conductor took advantage of the distraction you caused and tried to hit Billy, I think."

"Did anyone—shoot him?"

"No, though it was tempting." He saw the relief in her eyes and then she frowned.

"Where am I?" She attempted to sit up, but he tightened his grip on her good shoulder. "Where's the train?"

Bob approached them. "You feelin' better, ma'am? Them gunshots hurt like, uh, heck."

"Yes," Elizabeth agreed. "But Mr. Younger won't let me get up."

The bearded man turned to Logan. "It's done. Your share is packed. We divvied up the supplies this morning. You want me to help you get her on the horse?"

"Yeah." Logan eased Elizabeth onto the ground. "Try not to move your arm," he told her. "The bleeding hasn't stopped yet."

She dared a peek at her shoulder, then looked away. "Can you take me back to the train? I need to get to a hospital."

Logan moved to his horse and rearranged the packs to his liking. "Can't do that," he said. "Too dangerous."

She struggled to get to her feet, but her knees wouldn't hold her. She was freezing cold, too, she realized as she sank back onto the ground. Her arm throbbed painfully and she fought the nausea that threatened to overwhelm her. "I have to see a doctor."

"None of us can risk going into a town." Logan led his horse close to her. "Not yet." He put his foot in the stirrups.

Elizabeth grew even colder as she watched him mount the horse. Her horse was tied behind his. "You're leaving me here?"

He nodded toward Bob, who picked up Elizabeth and lifted her into Logan's arms. "Can you ride astride if you lean back against me?" the outlaw asked.

She tried to swing her leg over the horse's neck, but she jostled her injured arm in the process. Elizabeth took a deep breath and tried to deal with the pain. She didn't care what she had to do as long as she wasn't going to be left behind in these barren hills.

"Lean back," Logan repeated, settling her against his hard chest. "Better get as comfortable as you can. We've a long way to go."

The others gathered around for a brief goodbye. It was clear even to Elizabeth, who was feeling woozy again, that they were well prepared to go their separate ways. She had the impression they weren't planning to see one another again.

"You know how to find me," Bob said, clasping Logan's hand. "Good luck."

Logan cleared his throat. "And good luck to you."

"When you find Danny, tell him I said hello. I don't think he'll remember me, but you never know."

"He'll remember," Logan said. "I'll make sure of it." He raised his voice to the others. "Take care, boys!"

Billy grinned. "Don't worry about us."

The outlaw nodded. "Get out of here, all of you."

Elizabeth watched as the outlaws rode in different directions. The brothers stayed together. Logan turned his horse, and guided the animal over the crest of a hill. Every jolt of the horse caused a fresh wave of pain to radiate through her arm, but Elizabeth didn't make a sound. She willed herself to remain quiet, afraid that he would leave her if she became too much trouble. She concentrated on breathing, hoping to blot out the pain. She had no choice but to lean against Logan and trust that he would not let her fall.

She hated trusting him, but she had no choice. No choice but to believe he wouldn't dump her in this isolated place. She wanted to ask where they were going, but she couldn't overcome the pain long enough to speak. They were heading toward mountains. He had moved the horse into a trot. She knew he was trying to put as much distance as possible between himself and the train. A sheriff would come after them, no doubt. Three hours, Bob had said, and he hadn't sounded pleased. She guessed that wasn't much of a head start in the outlaw business.

Elizabeth closed her eyes against the bright sunlight as Logan kept the horses to a bone-jarring trot. The pain burned through her entire arm. She could no longer fight the dizziness, so she let Logan take her weight as she drifted in and out of consciousness.

He had to get out of there fast or they'd both be dead. Anyone who came after them would be happy to shoot them, and he wasn't convinced that Richardson wasn't far behind, either. If he cared about the woman, he would want her back.

Logan knew he needed to find shelter before night set in, so he pushed the horses harder than he wanted. He guessed the motion hurt the woman in his arms, but he tried to hold her as steady as he could. A fresh rivulet of blood leaked from the bandage, ran down her arm and dripped into a puddle on her dress. The sight made him sick, but he could feel her steady heartbeat under his arm. She was still alive. The wound wasn't a lethal one, but he'd seen lesser wounds go bad.

Many hours later, as sundown colored the horizon beyond the distant Salt Lake, Logan guided his horse up a narrow overgrown trail. He hoped to find shelter, since the mountains between Utah and Idaho had been explored by gold seekers for many years. There would be settlements along the trail between Brigham City and Pocatello, but he couldn't risk showing his face yet. He hoped the marshals would assume he'd headed east to

Green River country, but he couldn't afford to bet on
it.

The horse picked his way gingerly up the rocky hill-
side, Elizabeth's mount trailing behind. There was no
sign of anyone around, but Logan stopped the horses
and got his revolver out of the holster. Then he picked
up the reins again and started forward. The trail wound
higher, and as they rounded yet another turn, a ram-
shackle dwelling appeared on the edge of the ridge. It
appeared to be empty, but Logan wasn't about to take
any chances. He made his way carefully to the cabin
and paused a few yards from the open doorway.

"Hello!" he called.

Nothing but the wind answered the sound of his
voice. Splintered boards lay in front of the opening,
showing he was not the first person to need this place
for shelter. He'd lucked out.

"Elizabeth," he said, hoping to wake her. He wasn't
sure how he was going to get her down from the horse
without hurting her.

"Mmm," was her response. She burrowed into his
long coat, closer to the warmth of his chest.

"Lean forward," he told her. "Hold on to the saddle
horn for a minute. Can you do that, honey?" He moved
her away from him and helped her grasp the pommel
with her good hand. Her fingers were icy, all the more
reason to get her inside before dark. Logan dismounted, then reached up, grabbed her by the waist
and lifted her off the horse. Then he picked her up in
his arms and carried her to the shelter.

It was empty. He kicked aside the boards and carried Elizabeth inside. Hesitating before laying her
down, he finally chose an empty spot in the corner,

then took off his coat and placed it over her. "Stay here," he said unnecessarily. "I'll be right back."

"Don't," she said, looking at him with those blue eyes.

"I'll be back," he promised. "I won't leave you."

"Where are we?"

"Above the Bear River," he told her, standing up. "If we're not in Idaho then we're pretty damn close." He found water, took care of the horses and brought all of their belongings into the shack. He lit a candle and examined the inside of the miner's cabin. It wasn't much, just a lot of rough boards banged together. Room enough for one man to sleep and eat inside and nothing more. But it was out of the wind and there was water close by, so Logan couldn't complain. He assembled his camp stove and boiled water, knowing the time had come to clean Elizabeth's wound.

He found his whiskey bottle and fortified himself with a swig, then saved the rest for an antiseptic and some liquid comfort when this was all over. Armed with another strip of petticoat and his bar of soap, Logan took his knife and candle and set to work. He'd expected her to fight him, but she watched him carefully. She bit her lip and winced as he inspected the wound, but she didn't complain.

He gave her the whiskey bottle and helped her sit up so she could take a drink.

"Is it going to get any worse?" she asked tightly, clearly struggling to ignore the pain.

"No. Yes. I don't know." He looked down at her arm as if he could tell by looking at it. "The bullet went clean in and out, and I don't think it hit bone."

She winced again and took another drink of the whiskey. "I missed my train."

"There are others."

"For you, maybe." She protested when he took the bottle out of her hand.

"We're going to need this for disinfectant," he explained. "I'm going to put some powder in there and bandage it up. That's all I can do."

"I need a doctor."

"A doctor wouldn't do anything more than I've done." He eyed the bottle and reluctantly stuck the cork back in. He wouldn't mind a few more swigs, especially after pulling off the biggest job of his short outlaw career, but he needed to save the rest. He held the bottle up to the meager light of the candle and saw there was at least half left, so he uncorked it and took another draft.

"My turn," Elizabeth said, holding out her hand.

"I liked you better when you were unconscious," he muttered, passing her the bottle.

"Hey, I've had a bad day. Missed my train, got shot, arm hurts like hell. I'm not real crazy about 1886 so far." She put the bottle to her lips and drank two large gulps before he pulled it away.

"Go easy there, lady."

"As they say, 'The good ole days weren't all that good.'"

Logan snatched the bottle away, but not before wondering what the hell she was talking about. "Yeah, well, if you ask me, I'd say we're moving too fast. Used to be a man could live his life without a lot of interference."

"Anybody invented the telephone yet? I'd like you in my calling circle."

He touched her forehead but she wasn't feverish. "Can't hold your liquor, can you?"

"You ain't seen nothin' yet," she sang. He realized she was getting tipsy. She'd had a lot of whiskey on an empty stomach, plus she'd lost a lot of blood. "You have any codeine in that bag?"

"You need some food," he muttered.

"Good idea. I'll take a Big Mac and a large fries," she announced. "Screw the cholesterol! I'm on vacation."

He rummaged through the pack and handed her a hard biscuit. "Here. Chew on this. Might keep you from puking on my coat tonight."

Elizabeth nibbled on it and made a face. "I think you should have killed him."

"Who?"

"The bastard who shot me." With that, she closed her eyes and slid to the floor.

WHEN SHE WOKE, she was pressed against a man's warm, solid body. Gray morning light showed her she was in a small shack, the hard floor underneath her cushioned by some fabric. She lay on her back, her right arm firmly bandaged to her side to keep her from moving it. Logan was on her left, breathing softly on top of her head as he slept. Her arm ached and she had to go to the bathroom. She eased herself away from him and used her good arm to push herself to a standing position on legs that wobbled alarmingly. She was still wearing the calico dress over the pants she'd worn for riding.

A silly outfit, especially with only one sleeve left on the dress.

She tiptoed out of the cabin, her feet clad in the boots she'd tugged on yesterday. She vaguely remembered Logan cleaning her arm, but after that she couldn't remember anything. The door opened with a creak, but

Logan didn't stir as Elizabeth pushed it open farther and slid out into the chill morning air.

After some difficulty unbuttoning the pants, she managed to relieve herself behind a tree. She couldn't see much from the hill. They were on the side of a mountain, which didn't tell her anything. She'd never been much of a geography lover. Her classes in business administration and management were not going to come in handy in this century.

Elizabeth stumbled back to the shack. She really didn't feel very well. She managed to untie her boots and slip them off, then worked to take off the pants, too. She was hot and had no use for them.

She hesitated before entering the shack where Logan was still sleeping. She'd missed the train, she realized. She could take a horse and head down the mountain, but she would have no idea where she was going. Her right arm was injured and she couldn't shoot a gun with her left. She needed a hospital, but she may as well wish for a four-wheel-drive Jeep and a bottle of painkillers, for all the good it would do her. There was nothing to do but pray she would survive this. She didn't understand why she had been thrown back in time, especially when her life had finally taken a turn for the better.

She'd made herself into someone she was proud of, a woman who would deserve a prominent man like John Lovell. But she'd made a mistake by buying that book. It had set off a chain of events she wasn't sure she could stop, no matter how much she tried. Her body ached, but the effort to step inside was almost too much to make.

"Elizabeth?"

She turned as Logan filled the doorway. He looked exhausted. His gray eyes looked tired, and there were deep lines etched on either side of his mouth. He hadn't shaved for as long as she'd known him, which gave him the look of a true outlaw. As he stood there in dark pants and an unbuttoned flannel shirt, Logan looked like what he was, a man on the wrong side of the law.

"You could use a makeover," she said, suddenly feeling weak. She'd moved her body too much; the pain had started up again in earnest.

He frowned and touched her forehead with his large palm. "Burning up. I was afraid of that." He swept her into his arms and took her inside the dark room and laid her down on the makeshift bed. "Try to stay there. I'm going to get some water."

"Okay," she managed to whisper. She felt as if she had the flu. People died easily in this century. Maybe this is the way it was supposed to be. Maybe before you died, you got to spend some time in another life, kind of like visiting a foreign country.

He came back with a canteen full of water and a knife. "You real attached to this dress?"

"I hate it. Next time, tell Billy I want something that fits." She held her breath while he slit the fabric from the high neck to the waist. Underneath, she was wearing the white chemise, with its wide straps and narrow fringe of lace above her breasts. She shouldn't have felt embarrassed, but she did.

"I've got to cool you down," he explained.

"The wound's infected, isn't it?"

"Maybe, maybe not." He eyed the bandages. "I'll check it later. I've been trying to keep it clean."

"I know. It hurts." She didn't stop to wonder why she trusted him, but she did. There was no one else, and he hadn't left her when he could have. "Why didn't you leave me at the train?"

He wiped her hot skin with a wet rag and Elizabeth closed her eyes when the cool water drizzled down her face. "Maybe I should have."

"Then why?"

Logan took his time answering. "I had to make sure you would be all right," he admitted. "I couldn't leave you there to die."

"I could die here." She opened her eyes to look into his. He shook his head.

"I'm not going to let you die, Lizzie."

"No one calls me Lizzie." She closed her eyes again. It was too much of an effort to keep them open. "Never."

He chuckled. "I can't help it."

She tried to stay awake, but she felt herself slipping away. "If I die, you have to know my name. Elizabeth Anne Richardson, from Boston."

"I remember," he said, continuing to wipe her face with soothing motions. He moved the cloth to her neck and the base of her throat.

"I'm not from here," she managed to say, despite the pounding in her head. "I have to tell you—"

"Shut up, Lizzie," he said, his voice low. "Try to lay still for a while, 'til the fever goes down."

"It was 1970," Elizabeth remembered. "I was born in 1970."

"Sure," he agreed, wondering if she meant 1870 or if she was delirious. She looked older than sixteen, so he knew the fever had made her a little touched in the head. No matter, he decided. She'd been a little odd since she'd appeared in his hotel room. There were some odd characters out West, though. Some women did as they pleased and were damn proud of it, too.

She didn't protest as he cut more of the dress from her. The chemise kept her decent, though he tried to avoid looking at the swell of bosom above the white cotton. She was a tiny thing, but her breasts were full enough. He moistened the rag once again and laid it on her forehead. She'd fallen asleep, which was probably a good thing.

Logan sat back on his heels and took stock of the situation. He was sitting in a shack with an injured woman and forty thousand dollars of Crocker's money. The old bastard was most likely screaming about its loss, too. Logan grinned. No matter what happened, he'd gotten even with the railroad baron, and sometimes he thought that was all that mattered.

SHE CRIED OUT for the book, so he rummaged through her pack, found it for her and let her hold it to her chest with her uninjured arm. He sat with her all that day, leaving once to find something to eat. He shot a quail, which pleased him. The creek on the ridge below the shack looked too shallow to hold trout, but Logan was grateful for the plentiful supply of water. He wondered if the miner who'd built this place had had any luck.

Maybe he'd found his treasure and moved on, a richer man for having ventured into the mountains where Jim Bridger once made his fortune trapping.

Logan took care of the horses the best he could and hurried back to the shack. Lizzie was still asleep, but her cheeks were red and dry to the touch. He would give her another day, then he'd risk the ride to the next settlement. He didn't want to subject her to another long ride if he could prevent it.

He roasted the quail over a fire outside and saved the choice pieces for Lizzie, but when she woke up she didn't want food. He managed to get some more water into her, but that was all. That night, he slept by her again, waking often to wipe her face and neck.

He changed the bandage on her arm, though tears dripped from the corner of her eyes and into her hair as he checked the wound. When he didn't see any signs of infection, he could have cried himself, from relief.

As dawn broke over the mountains, Logan touched Lizzie's face with gentle fingers. Her skin was cool beneath his rough fingertips and she opened those blue eyes and smiled at him.

"Logan?"

"I'm here."

"Is it okay?"

"You're going to be fine," he said, knowing the words he spoke were true.

"Really?"

"Yeah." He touched her face again and she reached up with her free hand and took his.

"Thank you for taking care of me."

Logan looked at their clasped hands. He didn't want to want her. He didn't want to want any woman, but he couldn't help wanting this one. "My fault," he managed to say.

"No." She shook her head. "None of this has been your fault. You've done what you had to do, and I'm still alive."

"As soon as you're better, I'll see that you get to a train."

"I'd appreciate that." Elizabeth released his hand. "When do you think we can travel?"

He shrugged. "Wait and see."

"Where are we?"

"Near the Idaho border, in an old miner's shack."

"Will the law be looking for you?"

"Yes. But they'll have trouble tracking all of us through these mountains."

"Then you're safe here?"

"I think so. As safe as I can be." Logan looked down at the beautiful woman lying quietly on his coat and knew he wasn't safe at all. He didn't want to care for her. He wanted to find Danny, and already had been slowed because of the woman. He didn't know who she was, or how she had appeared in his life and he didn't care. All Logan Younger wanted was to reach down and take her mouth again. Instead, he stood up and ran a hand through his hair.

His skin burned where she'd touched him.

6

"I WISH YOU KNEW how to cook," Logan grumbled. He stirred beans in the metal pot over the campfire and frowned into the pot.

"I can cook," Elizabeth informed him. "But not outdoors."

"Can you make bread?"

She shook her head. She'd never understood the appeal of kneading dough. "Nope."

"Well, what *can* you cook?"

Elizabeth thought about that for a minute. She sat on the hard ground, with her arm bandaged close to her side, while Logan cooked the noon meal. She tried not to laugh at his grumbling, but it wasn't easy to keep a straight face. It was a beautiful day: she was alive and growing strong and Logan would soon take her to a train. He wouldn't rob it before he let her board, either. "Spaghetti and meatballs. Coq au vin. Vegetable lasagna. Linguini with pesto and garlic. Things like that."

"Foreign food?"

"I guess you could call it that." She would have to try to explain it to him. He would have to realize how important it was that she return to that hotel room in Salt Lake as soon as she could. They'd been heading in the wrong direction; it was time to turn around.

"Sounds fancy, anyway."

"Not exactly." Elizabeth leaned forward to watch him mutter over the steaming pot. "What else are you making?"

"I'll shoot a rabbit for supper."

She gulped, but knew better than to complain. She was damn lucky to have anything at all to eat in this isolated place. She would have died without Logan to take care of her. "Can I tell you a story?"

He turned to her and smiled. "I guess I can't stop you."

"Do you believe in ghosts?"

"Why? You seen an old gold miner wandering around here?"

"Come on, I'm serious."

He nodded. "All right. Ghosts, huh?" He mixed flour and water together to make a stiff batter. "Yeah, I guess so. There's some that say more than a few houses are haunted. And I've been in some places that make my own hackles rise."

"Do you think that people can predict the future?"

"No," he snorted. "I sure as hell don't."

This wasn't going to be easy, Elizabeth thought, not for the first time. She faced a man who lived a simple life. A life of survival and violence, of black and white and nothing in between. Would he believe her story? Would he be willing to help her? "What if I told you I was born in 1970?"

He gave her a sharp look, but his tone was casual as he answered, "You already did. Last night, when the fever had you."

"It's true, Logan. I really was born in 1970. I'm twenty-six. I was in the middle of visiting Salt Lake City in 1996 when—" she waved her hand around the shaded area where they sat "—all this happened."

"You expect me to believe this or are you just trying to keep me entertained while I'm cooking your dinner?"

"I'd like you to believe it."

He nodded. "Go on. I'm listening."

"I was in Salt Lake on business, at a conference. I went into an antique shop and bought some old books. One of them is the one I carry with me."

"The one you read to us from."

"Yes. I went to sleep reading it, and when I woke up, you were there and it wasn't 1996 anymore." She waited for him to say something, but he continued to stir the beans. "Well?"

He looked up at her and smiled. "You tell one hell of a story, Lizzie."

"It's not a story. It's true."

Logan's expression didn't change. He still looked amused as he gazed at her over the coals. "I guess this means you're not involved with that bounty hunter who's after my neck."

"Come on, Logan, give me some slack. I've got a big problem here."

"More than one, I'd say." He placed rolls of dough on top of the beans and set the lid on the pan. "What's going back to Salt Lake have to do with anything?"

"I think if I go back to where this, uh, accident happened, maybe there's a chance I can go back. The book must be the key, don't you see?"

"Then take the book and go to sleep."

"I tried that, but nothing happens. That's why I think the hotel room is the other part of the solution. Like some cosmic door."

"Coz-mic door," he repeated, staring at her. His face, still covered with that growing beard, was typically unreadable. The expression in his eyes was anything but serious. Elizabeth struggled to her feet and retrieved the book from the cabin. She sat beside Logan and opened it to the page where the wanted poster showed Logan's face.

"Is that you?"

"Could be," he admitted. "There's a definite resemblance."

"How long have you been robbing trains?"

"Almost a year now."

"Long enough to have your face in a book already?"

He studied the picture for a long moment. "This could be any one of my uncles, Lizzie."

"But it's not," she insisted. "It's you. Were your uncles in Utah?"

"No."

She pointed to the poster. "It says, Wanted in the State of Utah and Surrounding Territories right there."

He slammed the book shut. "I'm not an outlaw any longer."

"What's that supposed to mean?"

"It means I've quit. There's enough money now to—" He broke off.

"To what?"

Logan didn't answer the question. He took a stick and poked the coals.

Elizabeth thought for a minute. "I don't think you can just quit being an outlaw, can you?"

"I'm going to try."

"Well," she said softly, "I hope it works out for you."

"I'm not taking you back to Salt Lake."

"Then get me to a town where I can take a stagecoach, or something."

He shook his head. "Can't do that."

"Why not?"

"You'd have a posse after me in two minutes."

"I promise not to. My word of honor."

Logan lifted the lid of the pan and sniffed. "I sure wouldn't mind being rid of you."

"Does that mean you'll take me to a town?"

He spooned beans and biscuits onto two plates and handed her one. "Can you manage?" he asked, giving her a spoon.

"I think so." She had gotten better at using her left hand, but she was still awkward and clumsy. It was easier to eat with her fingers, but she didn't think she could eat beans that way.

"Let's see," Logan said later, when he had finished his plate. "You want me to take you to a town so you can go back to Lottie's hotel in Salt Lake City and use an old book with my picture in it to find a coz-mic door, is that right?"

"I know it sounds ridiculous."

"Lady, this past week has been nothing if not ridiculous. You scared the hell out of me when you got shot, but you're stronger than you look, so I guess that's going to turn out all right, after all. But this stuff about traveling from the future is too much for a man to understand."

"You don't have to understand," she pleaded. "You just have to help me."

"No," he said, looking at her with all amusement gone from his face. "I don't."

"Please. You're . . . all I have."

"Who is John?"

"My fiancé. John Lovell. How do you know his name?"

"You called for him when you were suffering from the fever."

That was strange. She didn't remember saying his name. "We're to be married in May. Next month."

"Yeah. I remember you said that once. That's why you want to get back to Boston."

"That's part of it, yes."

"Where does this John think you are?"

"I don't know. He must be very worried."

"Worried enough to send someone after you?"

"Maybe." She saw him tense and hurried to reassure him. "In 1996. They're not going to be able to find me, unless I'm already dead and this is some kind of dream." From the pain in her arm, she didn't think it was like any dream she'd ever had before.

"Neither one of us is dead." Logan winked at her. "Yet."

LOGAN STEPPED OUTSIDE into the dark night and lit his remaining cigar. The air smelled like rain, which didn't please him. While it might hamper anyone tracking him, it also slowed down his own escape. Not that he was going anywhere.

Elizabeth was inside. He'd given her privacy to make up her bed and crawl into it without him. Not that she had any nightclothes to change into, but he knew women liked their bedtime rituals.

Sarah had brushed her hair and rebraided it, unless he'd asked her to wait. He liked the way it spilled over his shoulders when she lay on top of his body. She'd been shy about loving him that way, but she'd been a virgin. A new bride, new to the ways of lovemaking those first years.

Those only years. Danny had been born nine months after the wedding. He was three when the trouble came. Three when his mother was shot down in a wheat field.

He took a deep drag of the cigar and closed his eyes to blot out the image that haunted his every waking moment. *It's over, Sarah. I got back what they owed us. Got back everything but your life.*

Logan opened his eyes and looked up at the night sky. The stars were covered with thick clouds and the wind smelled wet. The woman was healing. At least, her arm was. He wasn't too sure about her head.

He couldn't trust her to keep her mouth shut, not if she was crazy. He would have to get Danny first. He would have to keep her with him until he had Danny, until he was ready to disappear.

And what about her? Had she disappeared from her life in 1996? He couldn't believe he was considering the possibility that such a thing could really happen. Elizabeth thought she was telling the truth. Either that or she should be on the stage. The woman could make a fortune telling stories like that.

Unless it was true. He'd heard of strange things before, Indian stories of visions, Chinese beliefs in the afterlife. Something nagged him about that book, though. He'd have to look at it again. He chuckled to himself. Maybe its magic powers could take him to Pocatello. It would save him one hell of a ride across the mountains between here and Idaho country.

ELIZABETH WAITED for Logan to come inside. She didn't like lying in the dark alone. The shack was dirty and she was afraid that rodents, accustomed to wandering freely between the loose boards, would scamper over her body in the night. There were worse things to fear, she knew, but she felt safer with Logan beside her.

Sleeping with an outlaw had become her only source of comfort.

Her arm and shoulder hurt, but the pain wasn't as severe as it had been yesterday. She was young. She'd heal.

The bullet hadn't lodged in her skin. Which was supposed to be a good thing, Elizabeth understood. Logan had changed the bandage again before dinner. At this rate, she would wear no petticoat back to Salt Lake.

She'd been gone nine days. Nine days that John would have been looking for her. Nine days that her office would be without her. The place would be a mess. She'd have stacks of work to catch up on, and there was the grant for the new parking lot. Had she missed the deadline? Would her assistant, Christine, be able to do it without her help?

She would have to work night and day before the wedding. Maybe it was a good thing that they were only taking four days for a honeymoon. Elizabeth comforted herself with the thought of returning to Boston. She imagined walking into her apartment and checking her mail. Every day there were reply cards to the wedding invitations.

There had to be a way to prove it to Logan, but she didn't know how. There was no copyright date inside the book; that page must have been torn out, along with the author's name. How could she get him to believe her? She carried nothing with her from Massachusetts, no proof of who she used to be.

He had to take her back to Salt Lake City. It was her only chance to escape this beautiful but harsh land.

She heard Logan enter the cabin and prop the door shut. He sat down beside her and pulled off his boots. She was growing familiar with the nightly ritual. "Do you always sleep in your clothes?"

"No, but when I'm traveling it's easier."

"Can we wash clothes tomorrow?"

"Why?"

"We're filthy, that's why. We both smell like your horse."

He chuckled and lay down beside her. "In other words, you want me to wash the clothes. You can't lean over a creek one-handed."

"Whatever it takes," she replied.

"We're not spending any more time here," he said. "It's time we hit the trail."

Her heart lifted and she rolled onto her good shoulder to face him in the dark. "To Salt Lake?"

"No."

"Then where?"

"North, over the mountains to Idaho."

"Why?"

"That's not important."

Elizabeth thought for a moment. "Bob wished you luck in finding someone. Is the person you're looking for in Idaho?"

"You ask too many questions. Your arm must be better."

"You're not giving me answers."

There was silence as he turned toward her. "Shut up and go to sleep," he said, not sounding angry at all. "Do you have the book with you?"

"Yes. Under my pillow, which I thank you for stealing from the hotel, by the way. Not that I approve of stealing, of course."

"Of course." He sounded amused. "But you're glad you have a pillow?"

"Over and over again," Elizabeth answered. "Logan?"

"What?"

"I can't go to Idaho," she said.

"You don't have any say in the matter. A woman alone can't make it out here. Too dangerous."

Elizabeth thought about that for a few minutes. Logan was right. A one-armed woman had no business making her way in the mountains, even on the off chance she knew where she was going. She couldn't protect herself and most likely there were other men like that creep Parker who would be happy to take advantage of a woman alone. "Are there trains in Idaho?"

"Yes. Once we get there, I'll see that you get on a train. You can go anywhere you want."

"Promise?"

"You have my word, but there's a promise of your own I'll need before we leave here."

"What is it?"

"You're to stay with me until I tell you it's safe to go."

"How long?"

His voice was emphatic. "As long as it takes."

"Fair enough," she said. He could have left her at any point along the way, but he'd taken her up on his horse and ridden to safety. He'd bandaged her; he'd stopped the bleeding. He'd cared for her when she'd had a fever. He'd fed her and waited in this shack for her to be well enough to ride. "Why didn't you leave me, Logan? You've put yourself in danger because of me."

"It was my fault you were shot," he said. "I couldn't let you die."

Elizabeth moved to touch his hand. She could move her arm from the elbow, but it was painful. Still, she made the attempt to touch him. "Thank you," she whispered, realizing how much she owed this rough, bearded outlaw. He jerked his arm away and rolled onto his back.

"Go to sleep," he growled.

"I shouldn't thank you?" When he didn't answer, she sat up and leaned over him. "Why not?"

Logan, his eyes shadowed in the inky darkness, turned to look at her.

"Damn it," he said as he sat up and reached for her, cupping his hand behind her neck and bringing her to him. Elizabeth felt his lips touch hers, not an angry kiss like the first one. This kiss was something more. He was careful not to hurt her as he held her close to him, but his lips urged hers open, and when she obeyed, his tongue found hers and took her mouth completely. Elizabeth moaned, but she was powerless to move. His other hand supported her waist and kept her from falling. He kissed her thoroughly, as if he had been waiting to for a long time.

And Elizabeth didn't stop to wonder why she responded to him. They were alone, and she was not sure if she would ever be able to go home again. He was strong and kind and masculine. His lips were warm and demanding, his grip on her waist sending heat through her body. No one had ever kissed her like this before, and when he lifted his lips and moved to her neck, Elizabeth didn't protest. He trailed kisses along her cheek, to the edge of her eye, her forehead. It was as if he needed to taste each part of her face in order to believe she was real.

When he returned to her mouth, he kissed her parted lips softly. He ran his tongue along her lower lip and teased her with the sensuous motion. Elizabeth couldn't move, except to clutch his shirt with her free hand. She longed to touch him, but he held her away from him. Only their lips and his fingers on her waist joined them together.

For long moments, that was enough.

Logan lifted his mouth from hers. "It's not right that you touch me," he stated. Then he set her back on her blanket before climbing to his feet and leaving the shack.

Elizabeth sat alone for a while, until she could breathe normally again. She didn't know from where that passion had erupted, but she knew it was natural, considering that they were alone together.

Typical, understandable attraction. Nothing to worry about, she decided. Nothing that couldn't be dealt with in a mature manner.

But Elizabeth also knew for certain that Logan regretted it as much as she did. Her rapid heartbeat made her wound throb, so she got to her feet and went to the doorway. She couldn't lie down and pretend that nothing had happened. Would he ride away now, and leave her? She glanced around and saw him sitting by the dying coals of the campfire where he'd fixed the evening meal.

"Logan?"

He didn't look at her. "Go to bed, Lizzie. What happened won't happen again."

"I just—"

"Get out of here," he ordered.

There was no room for argument, she realized. Whatever his reasons for kissing her, he regretted the action. "Good night," she answered softly, hoping he would look up at her and smile.

Logan looked at her, but his expression was difficult to interpret. "You'll come to no harm from me."

"I know," she said, and turned to go inside the lonely little building. She curled up on the floor and pulled the blanket over her as comfort against the chilly night air. He'd kissed her, she mused, closing her eyes and willing her body to relax. It was the same kind of passion she'd seen in the movie *Butch Cassidy and the Sundance Kid.* Robert Redford had looked at Etta with passion like that.

And look where it got her. She'd followed her lover to South America and left when there wasn't a chance he would survive his dangerous life-style.

Elizabeth slipped her hand under the pillow and touched the old book. Despite the night air, the book was warm to her touch. It comforted her, and she fell asleep with her fingertips touching the cover.

THE NEXT MORNING, Logan led her to the small creek, where clear snow-cold water flowed above smooth rocks. "I don't know what good this is going to do," he said, hesitating before plunging the bundle of clothes into the icy water. "We're just going to get dirty again, soon as we leave here."

Elizabeth perched on a flat rock above the water. She was wrapped in a blanket, a shirt of Logan's covering her skin. "Wait until washing machines are invented. You just throw the clothes in with a cup of detergent and come back in forty-five minutes. Then you put the wet clothes in the dryer and fold them when they're done."

He frowned at her nonsense. "Do you have the soap?"

She handed him the bar and was careful not to touch the palm of his hand with her fingers. Logan pushed the clothes under the water and swished them around with a stick. One at a time, he took a piece of clothing and scrubbed it with the soap.

"You're pretty good at that," she said. The morning sun was bright and warm on her skin, and her arm, though tender, didn't throb unless she moved too fast.

"I've had to be," was his terse response. He grimaced as he soaped her underwear, then tossed it aside with the others to be rinsed. When he was done, he dropped the bar of soap into her hand.

"Have you ever been caught?"

"For what?"

"Robbing trains."

"No, not for that." He poked the soapy clothes with the stick and moved them through the clear water upstream.

"Then you've been to prison?"

"Yeah."

Intrigued, she wanted to find out more. His past interested her. His plan to quit being an outlaw was fascinating. His wife had died, there was a fortune in his saddlebags and he was searching for someone in Idaho. Another woman, perhaps? Most likely. "When?"

"A year ago."

"Did you escape?"

"No. I served my time." Logan squeezed the clothes, one by one, and set them on the rocks by his feet. "Damn, this water is cold!"

Elizabeth wondered if she dared ask what he'd done to go to prison. Robbery, she suspected. The man showed no remorse, and even looked as if he was having a good time when he was robbing that train a few days ago. Of course, growing up in the Younger family must have given him quite an education into a life of crime. She decided to ask one more question, one she had been wondering about since the morning of the robbery. "Why didn't you wear a kerchief over your face? You didn't care if they knew you?"

He smiled, a cold smile of satisfaction as he stood up and wiped his wet hands on his shirt. "They know me, all right. I want them to know."

"You're not afraid?"

"Lady, the railroad barons stole my father's land, and my land. They took away everything that ever mattered to me, everything I ever had." He bent down and picked up the balls of wet clothes. "All I've done is get back a little money, that's all."

"And now it's fair?"

"It'll never be fair, but I've done what I set out to do." He turned away and set off up the hill to the shack.

Elizabeth hurried after him, knowing she'd pushed him too far.

"HOW MANY DAYS?"

"Five. If all goes well." Logan adjusted the saddlebags, making sure the money was secure. He'd worked too hard to lose it all now. He turned to Elizabeth, who had followed him since sunup as if she thought he was going to ride off first time she turned her back. She was also determined to ride her own horse. "You sure you can manage?"

"Sure I'm sure," she said. She was back in her boy outfit again, now that the clothes had dried overnight. She'd tucked her hair under her hat and was wearing pants and a shirt. It didn't help. He still wanted her, with a fierce desire that wouldn't abate. He didn't care if she thought she was from the future, as long as she didn't talk about it all the time. He sure as hell didn't want her telling anyone else.

Not that he'd give her much of a chance. The less they were seen the better. He'd even burned the remains of the bloodied blue dress, knowing they could be identified if the word had spread that a woman in a blue dress had been part of an outlaw gang.

"Keep your hair up. If we meet anyone, I'll do the talking. If there's any shooting, pull your horse into the trees and get out of the way."

"Shooting? I thought we were all finished with that."

"Not yet. I'm a wanted man," he reminded her. "And you were part of a train robbery."

Her big blue eyes widened. "You think they're after *me?*"

Logan shrugged. "Hard to say. You ready?"

She nodded and moved her arm experimentally. "I think so. The sling you made feels good."

"Here." He lifted her into the saddle and helped her steady herself. He didn't touch her any longer than necessary, which took a great deal of restraint. He'd been without a woman for a long time. Through his own choice, he'd felt that taking another woman was giving dishonor to Sarah's memory.

Logan moved to his own horse and mounted. He had to start looking toward the future now. He would take another wife someday. But it was growing obvious that soon he would need to find a woman to give him comfort in physical ways. Before he did something stupid, like take a crazy woman, a woman who could get him hung, to bed.

A man who was concerned with staying alive would think twice.

7

SHE FOLLOWED HIM for mile after mile through the mountains over what seemed to be an old trail. They stopped briefly for a lunch of biscuits and apples, and then Logan put her on her horse and started off again.

The gelding appeared used to mountain travel. He picked his way across rocks and around fallen branches with little change in pace. Elizabeth's arm ached as the long day wore on, but she didn't complain. Every hour brought her closer to civilization and eventual freedom. She'd had plenty of time to think while riding, and she had spent hours convincing herself that there would be a way back, that she could still be married and she could be John's wife.

All her dreams could still come true.

She clung to that thought as her arm throbbed with every step the horse took, and she clung to the saddle horn. She stopped wondering where they were, she stopped caring. She prayed for Logan to stop, she prayed for sunset, when she knew he'd be forced to set up camp before dark. It was late afternoon when she watched him rein in his horse.

"Why are you stopping?" she called.

Logan looked over his shoulder at her and then turned away. "I'm thinking," he muttered.

Elizabeth urged the gelding forward, to stand beside Logan's big black horse on the crest of the mountain. Down below was a valley and a strip of blue river, but

Elizabeth focused on the cluster of buildings near the river. "Is that a town?"

He shrugged. "Yes. There are supposed to be small settlements all along this trail," he said. "Settlers have been passing through these mountains for years, heading to California and Oregon."

"Are we going down there?"

"That's what I'm considering." He sighed, took off his hat and ran a hand through his hair before setting the hat back on his head. "It should be safe. The robbery took place five days ago. That's enough time to get news, but we need supplies. We don't have enough food for four or five days' travel."

Elizabeth gazed down at the group of buildings huddled against the base of the mountain. "Do you think they have a store?"

"They'll have to have something."

"I hope you're right." She was tired of biscuits and beans.

Still he hesitated. "I can't be sure it's safe. I've never been this route before."

"Do we have any other choice?"

"Maybe not."

"Unless I go down instead. I wouldn't be recognized. You could tell me what to buy."

Logan bit back a smile. "I don't think that would work."

"Why not?"

"I can't let you go down there without knowing what kind of place it is. People get real suspicious of strangers." He glanced at her arm, then frowned when he studied her face. "You're in pain. Why didn't you say something?"

"I want to get to Idaho as much as you do."

"Dead or alive?"

"Pain's not going to kill me," she argued. "What are we going to do about going into that town?"

"Keeping your mouth shut would be a good start," he suggested.

Elizabeth envisioned soft beds, clean sheets and homemade apple pie. "Can we stay overnight?"

"No. We'll make camp on the next ridge. We're going to go in and get out without attracting too much attention." He slid off his horse, took some money out of his saddlebag and tucked it into his vest.

"Aren't you nervous carrying all that money around?"

Logan mounted his horse. "Yes, ma'am," he said. "I'm scared to death. Which is why I have a gun and you don't."

"Maybe I should," she said. "Have a gun, I mean."

"And how are you going to shoot it with your left hand?"

"I could hold it and look menacing."

"I told you, Lizzie, when you pick up a gun, you'd better be prepared to use it." Once more, he looked down at the cluster of buildings and frowned. "Maybe we won't run into any trouble. Just get in, get out and disappear into the mountains again."

"With that beard, you don't look like the man in the wanted poster," she said. "But you might try to look a little more friendly and less like you're ready to kill someone."

He tipped his hat. "Thanks for the advice."

"Anytime." Elizabeth braced herself for a hard ride down the mountain. It had been a long time since she'd seen people other than Logan Younger and his band of outlaws.

They rode side by side through the narrow dirt street.
Elizabeth glanced around, but the place didn't look as
if there was much going on. They passed a saloon, its
door propped open to let in fresh air. Sounds of laughter and partying came from the building, but no one
stood in the doorway to look at the newcomers to town.
A crude sign above a large wooden building said Preston General Store, leaving Elizabeth to wonder if Preston was the name of the town or of the store's owner.
They stopped at the hitching rail in front of the building and Logan dismounted. He considered the saddlebags, then, swearing under his breath, handed Elizabeth a revolver. "I guess I don't have any choice."

Elizabeth took the gun and held it awkwardly in her
left hand. "What do you want me to do?"

"Pull the lever back, like I showed you, and shoot
anyone who touches my horse. Can you do that?"

She gulped. "I can try."

"Ten minutes," he said. "Keep your hair covered and
try not to kill anyone until I come back."

Logan went into the store and approached the
wooden counter warily. An old man got out of his chair
and stood behind the cash register. "You want somethin'?" he asked, his glance taking in Logan's dusty
clothes and the holster under his vest.

"Supplies," Logan said, then remembered Lizzie's
advice to be more friendly. "Nice day."

"Yeah. Real nice. What'd ya have in mind?" The old
man took a rifle and moved it to within sight, a warning to Logan that he was prepared for trouble.

So much for being nice. He told the storekeeper what
he wanted and pulled a couple of bills from his pocket
to show he was ready to pay for the supplies. "I'm not
looking for any trouble," he said.

The man didn't answer. Instead, he assembled the food in a box and waited. "That it?"

"Throw in some of those licorice whips," Logan said. "How much?"

"Twenty dollars oughta do it."

Logan whistled under his breath and dropped the money on the counter. He wasn't the only robber in Utah, that was certain. "Pleasure doing business with you."

"We don't like trouble, mister," the storekeeper warned.

Logan picked up the box. "I'm not real crazy about it myself," he drawled, and turned to head for the door.

"Stop right where you are," the man said.

Logan heard the dangerous click of the rifle and stopped in his tracks. He didn't have much choice. His hands were still clutching the box. He'd be dead before he dropped the box, pulled his gun and turned to fire. He kept his voice casual. "You have a problem?"

The old man cackled. "No, I can't say as I do." Logan heard footsteps as the man shuffled across the floor. He poked the rifle between Logan's shoulder blades. "*You* have one, though. There was a marshal through here two days ago, looking for someone who has the bad habit of robbing the Southern Pacific Railroad. An outlaw." He cackled again. "He said there was one hell of a reward."

"You have the wrong man."

"Mebbee. Mebbee not. Don't matter none. You have the look of a man who's wanted for somethin'." He prodded Logan's back with the rifle. "Go on now, nice and steady. We're gonna head next door and lock you up 'til I can figure out what to do with you."

Logan gripped the wooden box and moved toward the door. There wasn't much else he could do with the barrel of a rifle in his back. He should have known better than to come into a town. He was used to traveling light, to avoid this kind of problem. "Traveling light" did not mean traveling with a woman.

They slowed you down and made you stupid.

And Logan, pushing the door open and stepping out into the late-afternoon sun, couldn't have felt any more stupid.

Elizabeth gave him an odd look, then her eyes widened as she noticed the gun. "What—"

Logan ignored her, turning to his left as the old man prodded.

"Nice 'n easy," he said, chuckling. "Don't want this rifle to go off by accident." He looked up at Elizabeth. "You with him, boy?"

"Yeah," she replied, keeping her voice low. "What'd he do?"

"You're keepin' bad company." His eyes narrowed speculatively as he eyed the sling that cupped her arm. "Mebbee there's a reward for your skin, too. You been shot in a robbery lately, lad?"

Elizabeth tried not to show her fear. "You're barking up the wrong tree, old man." She nodded toward Logan. "He's no outlaw."

"We'll just have to see about that."

Elizabeth felt a flash of fury at the sight of a gun nudging Logan's back. She couldn't let him be taken away like this. He might be an outlaw, he might be a man with a reputation for trouble and a name that would go down in history, but he didn't deserve to be locked up in this dirty town. And she damn well wasn't going to accompany him and try to explain 1996 to some county judge.

"I don't want any trouble," she warned the store-keeper, lifting the revolver with her left hand. It shook, so she steadied it with her right hand. She couldn't move her arm too far, but she realized she could point the gun in the old man's direction well enough.

Logan froze, still holding the box of supplies. The color drained out of his face as he watched her pull back the safety catch. "Don't do it," he begged.

The old man sensed that the power had shifted to the youngster with the shaking revolver. "Looks like we have ourselves a standoff," the man drawled.

She held the gun as steady as she could and kept it pointed at the old man's heart. "I've never shot a gun before," she admitted. "I don't know what I'll hit, but I do know that I paid good money to hire this man to take me over these mountains to . . . Wyoming," she explained, trying to keep her voice sounding as deadly as possible. *You are Sharon Stone, you are Clint Eastwood, you are John Wayne,* she told herself. "And one old man isn't going to screw it up."

When the man hesitated, Elizabeth added, "Ask yourself, do I feel lucky today?"

Logan groaned. "Damn it, man. Just put down the rifle before the boy kills us both."

The storekeeper lowered the rifle and spat a wad of tobacco in the dirt at his feet. "Don't want no trouble."

Logan turned around and thrust the box into the man's arms. "Hold this," he ordered as the rifle fell harmlessly to the ground. The man followed Logan to the horse, where he loaded the supplies onto Elizabeth's horse. When he was done, he walked over to the rifle and opened it, dropping the bullets into his palm and handing the rifle back to the man. "We're leaving. We're not bothering you or anyone else along this river. You got that?"

He nodded. "Guess I misunderstood," he said, eyeing Logan's easy handling of the revolver.

Logan nodded. "I won't take kindly to being followed."

Once again, the man spat in the dust. "Everyone's drunk, anyway."

The outlaw untied his horse and swung into the saddle. He looked at Lizzie, who still looked as if she was going to shoot. "You can give me the gun," he said, holding out his hand. "Nice and easy, boy."

She did as she was told, but she didn't take her gaze from the old man who stood watching them, his empty rifle in his hand. She was pleased with herself. Not because she'd held a gun on a man, but because she'd defended herself and the man she'd grown to respect. She was accustomed to negotiating and problem solving—she'd even led workshops on the subjects—but she'd never been able to look at someone giving her a hard time and say, "Ask yourself if you feel lucky today."

Boy, was she glad she'd seen *Dirty Harry*.

Logan tipped his hat. "Nice doin' business with you." He turned his horse to head north, out of town. "Come on," he urged Elizabeth. "Let's get the hell out of here before he decides to holler for help."

They trotted out of town, but saw no one else as they hurried the horses along the dirt street. Logan kept the horses at a fast trot while they crossed the valley, but slowed them to a walk as they approached the mountains. He said nothing, and Elizabeth knew he was concerned. Her arm ached from the jolting trot, but she didn't say a word. She knew they could be followed, and it was growing darker by the second. Clearly, Logan was trying to put as much space as he could between them and any curious townspeople, which was fine with her. The sooner they disappeared into the mountains the better, and they both knew it.

"I DON'T LIKE THIS," Logan muttered. They had steadily climbed up the side of the mountain, along a narrow trail that didn't look as if it got much use.

"Do you know where we're going?"

"North."

"Duh." They'd been going north all along. Now they were fast approaching the top of the ridge that ran along the top of the mountains. "I meant tonight," she said, "not in general."

"We'll make camp soon."

"Do you think it's safe to stop?"

"No choice. There's not going to be enough moonlight to see where we're going."

"Oh." The woods looked scary in the semidarkness. She was sure that wild animals were going to lunge out, but her horse kept moving along, his ears pricked to catch every sound. She liked the horse. He hadn't given her any trouble and just kept putting one hoof in front of the other, day after day. "Does my horse have a name?"

Logan turned around, his expression exasperated. "Not that I know of."

"I'm going to call him Clint." She patted his neck. "I don't know why I didn't think of it before."

The outlaw ignored her. He didn't seem too eager to talk. She wondered if his pride was injured. After all, she'd saved him from jail. The thought pleased her the more she thought about it. She wished she could call someone and tell them what she'd done. Her assistant would appreciate the story the most. She wasn't sure if John would approve, though.

Logan's horse picked his way along the ridge until Logan guided him off the trail and through the thick trees. He stopped in a small open area, large enough only for the horses and a small camp. Logan dismounted and tied his horse to a nearby branch, then stepped over to Elizabeth to help her from the saddle.

"We won't risk a fire," he said, dropping his hands from her waist as quickly as he could.

"What did you buy?"

"Keep your voice down," he warned. "I'm not real happy about what happened today."

She watched as he unbuckled the saddle and slid it from Clint's back. "He said everyone else in town was drunk."

"He could have been lying."

Elizabeth followed him while he took care of the horses. The only time they had stopped was at small streams to give the animals a drink, but there was no water here on the ridge. Young grass shoots would be the horses' only dinner. They deserved better than that, but Logan couldn't take any chances. Not in the dark. Elizabeth seemed determined to stay within an inch of him at all times, but he ignored her.

"What's the matter?" she asked. "Are you mad?"

"About what?"

"Today."

He brushed past her and unbuckled the saddlebags. He withdrew some cheese, bread and sausage, then sat down on the grass. Elizabeth sat across from him, crossed-legged. He pretended he didn't hear her groan when she sat down. He'd ridden her hard today. He wasn't proud of it.

He took his knife and sliced a hunk of cheese and handed it to her. He did the same for the sausage, then ripped off a chunk of thick bread for each of them.

"Thank you," she said.

"You're welcome." He tossed the canteen to her. "Make it last till morning."

"All right."

Logan watched her take a dainty sip of water. She was getting better maneuvering with that left arm. He'd have to change the bandage on her other arm tonight. He'd learned the hard way that wounds healed only if kept clean and dry, though a lot of people didn't necessarily believe that.

She took another bite of sausage and chewed. "This is a nice change."

"It'll do," he agreed.

"You still mad about that old man?"

"I should never have gone into that town."

Elizabeth smiled at him. "We made it."

Logan glared at her. "We're both lucky we didn't get shot. Your gun was shaking so hard, I thought I'd taken my last breath on this earth. There's a hair trigger on that Colt. I never should have given it to you," he muttered.

"And where would you be if I hadn't done some quick thinking?"

"You're dangerous. More dangerous than I thought. I can't believe I gave a crazy person a gun."

She frowned back at him. "You're just mad because a one-armed *woman* saved your ass."

"Watch your mouth, lady."

Her chin lifted. "No. I don't have to 'watch' anything. I talked that man out of locking you up. My gun, shaky or not, convinced him to let you go. You'd still be there if it wasn't for me."

"*Do you feel lucky today?* That was supposed to scare him?"

"It made him think twice."

"Shut up."

"No. I don't know why—"

"*Shut up,*" he hissed, and clapped one hand over her mouth. Elizabeth struggled. She didn't know he had taken her conversation so seriously.

He whispered into her ear, his warm breath tickling her skin. "There's someone coming. Stay down." He released her and handed her one of his revolvers. "Here we go again." He sighed. "Don't use it unless you have to."

"Meaning?"

"If someone shoots me, kill him. Understand?"

She nodded. He crept to his belongings and picked up his rifle, then motioned for her to hide behind a rotting log. They lay there together, listening for a sound in the darkness. At least they'd had time to finish dinner. She might have shot someone for a cup of coffee, though.

Elizabeth strained to hear any sounds other than normal night sounds. Odd how accustomed she'd become to sleeping in the woods. She tried to picture camping with John, but couldn't. Her future husband was a brilliant man, but he'd never been forced to survive on his own. She turned her head slightly so she could observe Logan's expression. He looked determined to protect them from whatever danger lurked out there.

Elizabeth peered into the night until her eyelids grew heavy. She struggled to stay awake, reminding herself that she might be in danger and would need to be alert. But the long day caught up with her and, promising herself that she would simply rest, she leaned her arm on the log, put her head down and drifted off into an exhausted sleep.

She awoke as Logan took her in his arms and carried her to a blanket spread over the pine needles. She blinked and tried to see him in the dark. "What happened?"

"We have company. It's all right," he said, and covered her up with another blanket. "Get some rest."

He didn't have to tell her twice.

Logan stood over her for a long moment, then joined Billy at the small fire they'd built. Logan opened the whiskey bottle. "I thought you were headed to Green River."

"Not yet." Billy said. "I'll backtrack and take the main trail to Bear Lake tomorrow. I couldn't leave without knowin' you and the woman were okay. I hung around here hopin' I'd get word or see you pass through."

Logan frowned. "What else?"

Billy hesitated. "There's word that a marshal is lookin' for you. For us, I mean."

"I heard."

Billy grinned. "Heard you ran into a little trouble in town this afternoon."

"Where were you?"

"In the saloon. There was a burial today and the men in town spent all day drinkin'."

"All except the old man that owns the store. He held a gun on me and was ready to wait for the reward money. Is there any kind of law in that town?

"No, not that I could figure out. Closest law is still back in Brigham City, and they're probably still mad about the train, but that doesn't mean they're gonna chase after you, at least not this far."

"Yeah." Logan grinned with satisfaction. "That was one hell of a finish to a life of crime, wasn't it?"

His friend nodded. "I'm glad it's over, I've got to admit."

"Me, too."

Billy gestured toward the sleeping woman. "What about her?"

Logan shrugged. "The gunshot wound is healing."

"That's not what I meant. What are you gonna do with her?"

"Take her with me, get rid of her in Pocatello. She'd scream her head off if I left her now."

"You still think she's crazy?"

Logan thought about that for a long moment. "She thinks she dropped in here from 1996, Billy. How crazy is that?"

His eyes widened. "Gawd!"

"She keeps talking about going back to Salt Lake and seeing if she can find some kind of door—coz-mic door, she says—to take her back. Says the book with all the pictures in it is the reason she's here."

"Where's that book now?"

"She usually sleeps with it, but not tonight." Logan stood up and went to the saddlebags. "Here," he announced, holding up the book. "You want to see it?"

"No!" Billy stood up and took a step back. "Don't get that thing near me."

Logan held it between two fingers and sat down at the fire. "Maybe you should lay off the whiskey."

The older man sat down, but kept an eye on the book. "You think it has powers?"

"No." He handed his friend the bottle. "There's not much left."

Billy took the bottle and held it up to the light. "There's enough," he declared. He took a drink then shook his head sadly. "You've got your work cut out for you, Logan. Draggin' a crazy woman over these mountains, dodgin' bounty hunters and findin' Danny..."

"Is Richardson anywhere around?"

"Haven't heard. It's like he's disappeared. I don't like it."

"I don't, either. He's like a rattlesnake, all coiled up behind a rock."

"Well, watch where you step," Billy advised. He looked over to Elizabeth, still sleeping peacefully in the shadows. "A woman who looks like that won't go unmarried long, especially around here."

"Meaning?"

"Well, how crazy can she be? A lot of men would be glad of the company."

Logan frowned, remembering old man Parker's eager, beady eyes. "Stay away from her."

His friend looked horrified. "I'm not talkin' about *me*, Logan! Gawd! It's you, boy. You're gonna need a wife where you're goin'. You think there's a lot of women in Montana just waitin' to be a wife and mother to a wanted man and his little boy?" He shook his head. "So what if she's crazy? Ranchin' in Montana'll make her crazy, anyway."

Logan chuckled. "You've got a point," he agreed, grateful for the company and the warmth of the whiskey in his belly. It had been one hell of a day. "She's stronger than she looks."

Billy nodded. "I don't doubt that. Most women are, I've learnt."

"True."

The old man set the bottle on the ground and stretched out. "We'd best get some rest."

Logan nodded, then waited for his friend to start snoring. He'd risked a small fire, after Billy had assured him there was no one in town sober enough to trail a couple of travelers into the mountains. Logan opened the book to the page that showed the wanted poster. He'd wanted to study it without Elizabeth's interference. He'd wanted to think about what she had to say. He'd given it a lot of thought today, and he couldn't figure out what bothered him so much about the sketch.

The book just looked like any old book, Logan figured. He leaned closer to the flame and tried to read the words underneath the picture in the wanted poster. *Wanted in the State of Utah and Surrounding Territories.*

A cold chill ran down his spine, and he forced himself to read the words again. He tipped the book closer to the light and squinted over the words. He didn't want to believe what he read, because believing was too damn hard.

Wanted in the State of Utah, the book said. Trouble was, Utah wasn't a state yet. Whoever wrote the book was mighty optimistic. Or careless.

Unless the book had been written after Utah gained statehood. Logan closed the book and returned it carefully to Elizabeth's bag. There wasn't much there. Just a small amount of clothing and the paisley shawl. She'd been wearing a nightgown when he'd first seen her. Nothing else.

Which didn't prove a damn thing.

Logan kicked dirt on the fire and took his bedroll over to Elizabeth's side. He'd grown used to sleeping beside her. He liked waking with her warm body pressed against his side. Sometimes in the dawn, he would lie there for long, extra minutes just so he could enjoy listening to her breathing.

He would leave before she could wake up and discover herself curled against him. He suspected she wouldn't appreciate the knowledge. Just as he didn't appreciate knowing he could be dealing with a woman from the future.

The thought gave him chills once again.

8

ELIZABETH AWOKE with a start. Something felt wrong. She kept her eyes closed and listened. She heard nothing but a faint birdcall. That was the trouble. The silence. She opened her eyes and sat up with a cautious motion. The clearing was quiet and empty.

The sky was overcast above the towering pine trees, so there was no way to tell how long the sun had been up. There was no fire, although she saw the remnants of one. Logan was nowhere to be seen, and when she looked over at the horses, his black horse was missing. Another, a large chestnut with one white forelock, was tied beside Clint.

Her stomach tensed. They had been followed. But where was Logan? Had something happened to him? She vaguely remembered him carrying her last night. She didn't remember anything more. Maybe he'd been caught, after all. Or maybe he'd gone off to hunt for something for breakfast, or to find water. He would come back, she told herself. He had to.

Elizabeth tossed the blanket off and stood up. If she was alone, she'd damn well better figure out what to do about it. She'd slept in her riding clothes, with her boots still on, so it was convenient to slip into the woods for a little privacy. For a woman who had never been a Girl Scout, she was managing okay, she thought. She longed for flush toilets and hot showers, perfumed soap and thick bath towels, mirrors and lipstick and a decent hairbrush.

When she returned to the camp, she heard a man swearing. It wasn't Logan's familiar voice, but one with more of a Western twang. She'd heard that voice before, though the string of swearwords was an original combination.

She stood on the edge of the clearing and watched Billy struggle with his boots. "Billy?"

He looked up and relief crossed his face. "Well, damn, Miz Lizzie! I thought I'd lost you! I shoulda woke up early like, but I guess I drank too much whiskey last night."

"You were the one following us?"

"Yes, ma'am. I've been mighty worried." He slapped his hat onto his head and looked toward the cold camp fire. "Guess Logan didn't eat."

"Where is he?"

Billy shrugged. "Gone to look around. He told me last night to look after you 'til he got back."

"But when is he coming back?" He hadn't left her. He couldn't have left her, she told herself.

"Don't know, but I sure hate to think what he'd say if I'da lost you." Billy shuddered. "How's that arm doin'?"

"I think it's going to be all right." She slipped her arm out of the sling and tried to straighten her elbow. Her upper arm, with its ugly gash, was still swollen and sore, but the pain wasn't as bad. "It's been six days now. Why are you here?"

Billy crouched and began to assemble a stack of kindling into a fire. "Guess I'm a worrier."

"Is there anyone following us? Do you think you're in danger?"

The older man put a match to the wood and waited for it to catch. "Hard to tell. Logan's like a brother to me. I don't want anything to go wrong. There's a mighty eager marshal roamin' the border, and I've no urge to meet up with him."

"You think he's close by?"

Billy winked at her. "I think he passed on by here, while you was hidin' somewhere nursin' your arm."

"Is he the bounty hunter you thought was in Salt Lake?"

"No." Billy frowned. "Haven't heard nothin' 'bout him since."

"Maybe he wasn't really there."

"Mebbee." But he didn't sound convinced. Elizabeth watched him fix a pot of coffee and set up the skillet for breakfast. "You learnt how to cook yet?"

"No."

"Well, sit down and watch an expert. We'd better eat quick—no tellin' when Logan will get back and want to move out of here."

"We're too close to town, aren't we?"

"Lady, this ain't nothin'."

"It's not?"

"Nope. We've had worse times."

Elizabeth waited, not sure whether or not she wanted to hear about the "worse times." Hiding out on a mountain while the law was after her was the worst thing she'd experienced in her adult life. Here she'd thought that once she turned eighteen and was in control of her own life at last, she would not allow anything to go wrong.

And that belief had held true for eight years, until now.

"What kind of worse times?" she asked, scooting closer to the warmth of the fire as she watched the middle-aged outlaw slice chunks of bacon into the skillet. The aroma made her stomach growl.

"Fightin' the railroad wasn't no picnic," Billy drawled. He picked up a leather glove and shook the metal coffeepot.

"Do you mean robbing trains?"

"No. We fought the railroad men out in California. They came to Logan's farm and we were waitin' for them."

"Why did they come to Logan's farm? To arrest him?"

"Nope. They took all our land and sold it. They'd promised we could buy it when they got the deed from the government, and they changed their minds." He winked at her, and poured coffee into tin cups. "After we'd improved it, farmed it, for years. There wasn't a gol-dang thing we could do."

Elizabeth took the cup he offered. "You fought them?"

"Yes, ma'am. And we killed a few of 'em, too. Didn't make much diff'rence, though."

"Why not?" She sipped her coffee and waited for the rest of the story.

He poked the bacon with his knife. "Law was on their side."

"What happened to your farms?"

"Gone. Half a lifetime of hard work gone, sold to make rich men richer."

"And that's why you rob the railroad."

Billy got to his feet and rummaged through his saddlebags. "Yes, ma'am. You hungry?"

"Yep. What are we having? Bagels? Dunkin' Do-nuts? A croissant?"

"Huh?"

"I'm just joking." Elizabeth sighed. "Biscuits, right?"

"How many?"

"Four." He took fistfuls of biscuits and tossed them on the bacon. No one worried about cholesterol or fat grams, she realized. They ate what they could travel with. They ate whatever was available and nothing more. "What are you going to do with your share of the money?"

"I'm headin' to Wyoming, I think. I passed through Green River—ever been there?"

"No."

"Well, I passed through there a few years back and liked what I saw. I'm guessin' I've got enough money in my saddlebags to buy a small place and raise a few head of cattle."

"Then you're finished with being an outlaw, too?"

He chuckled. "None of us were *outlaws*, not at first. We were just men tryin' to git back what was owed us. And we did it, too. Long as we can stay out of jail—"

Just then, Logan rode into camp, cutting off Billy's words. Elizabeth looked up at him and smiled with re-lief. He looked tired, as if he'd been riding for hours, but the black horse didn't look sweaty. Logan nodded to Elizabeth, but spoke to his friend.

"I could sure use a cup of that," he said, tilting his hat off his forehead. He dismounted, tied his horse and ap-proached the campfire. He nodded with approval when he saw the small amount of smoke coming from the flames. Billy found another cup and handed it to him.

"I'll throw some more of this here bacon in," he said. "I see you bought supplies before you was captured by old man Preston."

"Don't remind me," Logan drawled. He sat down beside Elizabeth and poured himself a cup of coffee. "Lizzie here is a bit wobbly with her aim."

"I didn't shoot anyone," she answered.

"Thank the good Lord," he muttered.

"Are you still upset about that? After all, you're the one who gave me the gun and told me to—"

Billy interrupted the argument. "You see anything this mawnin', Logan?"

He shook his head. "No. This trail follows the ridge north. There's no sign of anyone having been through here for a while, no sign of anyone coming from town, either. We'll eat and get on our way." He glanced over to Elizabeth. "I'd better change that bandage before we leave."

"Okay." Elizabeth gulped. She knew that keeping the wound clean was crucial, but the process was anything but comfortable and she dreaded it. They ate breakfast quickly, with Billy cooking extra helpings for Logan and himself. While Billy packed up the horses, Logan heated water.

"Take your arm out of the shirt," he said, waiting for her to comply.

She managed to unbutton the shirt and ease her arm from the sleeve. Underneath, she wore the cotton chemise, which covered her chest, but she still didn't like being exposed. She kept the other half of the shirt on, and Billy tactfully stayed on the other side of the clearing.

Logan unwound the bandage and washed the wound. "Look," he told her, pointing to the place where the bullet had entered. "No poisoning."

"It's still swollen."

"That's natural," he assured her. "But you're young and it's healing just fine."

"I got some of that Dr. James Powder," Billy called. "You want it?"

"No!" Then Logan lowered his voice so only Elizabeth could hear. "I don't trust those quack remedies," he said. "My mother used to believe in soap and water."

"She was right. I don't know if germs have been discovered here yet, but keeping medical equipment sterile prevents infection."

He gave her an odd look. "How would you treat a gunshot wound in, uh, 1996?"

Elizabeth stared at him. He was actually discussing it as if he believed her. "You believe me?"

"I asked you a question. I'm not talking about whether it's true or not."

"The area would be cleaned, of course. Probably x-rayed—that's where a picture of the bone is taken so doctors can see if anything's broken—and I'd be on some sort of antibiotic." She winced as he began to wind the clean strip of petticoat around her arm.

"Yeah? What's that?"

"Medicine to prevent bacterial infection."

He nodded.

"A pill," she explained, trying to ignore the pain in her arm. "Or a shot."

"And that works?"

"Yes. I manage a health clinic in Boston. When I get back, I'll have one of the doctors look at this and make sure everything's okay."

He tied it neatly, helped her with her shirt, pulled her sleeve down to her wrist and sat back on his heels. "You really believe you can make it back?"

Elizabeth nodded. "As long as I have the book, I have to believe it."

He cleared his throat. "I looked at that book last night."

"Where is it now?" she asked anxiously.

"Back with your things," he assured her. "Nothing happened."

"Did you feel how warm it was? And the vibrations?"

He gave her a pitying look. "No. It just felt like any old book." He stood up and watched as she put her arm in the sling. "Elizabeth—"

She looked up at him. "What?"

"When did Utah become a state?"

She tried to remember what she'd read in the tourist guide in her room. "It's not?"

"No."

Elizabeth wished she'd paid more attention to United States history when she was in school. "I'm not sure. I read that the Mormons had to give up polygamy before they could become a state. I think it was 1896." She grinned. "Ten years from now. You heard it here first."

He didn't smile. "You're lucky you're such a strong woman," he said, nodding toward her arm. "Not many could travel with an arm like that."

"I've always had a high pain threshold," she said. *And a strong reason not to waste time.*

"What's that?"

"I mean, I can take a lot of pain."

"You're going to have to," Logan said flatly. He stood up and looked down at her. "This isn't going to get any easier, and we've got three hard days of riding to do. I hope you can keep up."

"I can keep up."

He nodded. "Let's get started, then."

Elizabeth started to struggle to her feet, but Logan reached down and gave her his hand. She put her hand inside his and let him help her stand up. His skin was warm, his fingers strong around hers. She had the strangest urge to hold on to that hand for hours. There was such strength radiating from him, she knew she would be safe whenever he was near.

She'd never felt that way before, and when he released his hand and turned away, Elizabeth stood transfixed for a long moment and tried to gather her thoughts. She made herself remember she was getting married soon. She had no business thinking about the outlaw's hands, or admiring the outlaw's shoulders or enjoying the capable way he rode a horse and handled a Colt revolver—not especially valued skills at the end of the twentieth century, but she was grateful for them now. Fate had dumped her in this strange place, but had also given her a man strong enough to help her through whatever she faced while she was here.

LOGAN DIDN'T LIKE the looks of the dark clouds building above the mountain peaks. Up until now, they'd been lucky in having the rain hold off. But if he was any judge, he'd guess their luck was over. At least with the weather. He looked over his shoulder to make certain Elizabeth was still following. That gelding of hers liked to take his sweet time and Elizabeth didn't know enough to keep him moving as fast as he ought to be moving.

She didn't notice him turn around. She looked tired, and he could see she was leaning hard on the saddle horn. That old coat Bob had given to her hung almost to her knees; with her hair tucked under her hat, she looked mighty pathetic, like some disillusioned youngster on his first adventure. They'd only stopped once more, to water the horses and eat, and then he'd lifted Lizzie into the saddle and led her back to the barely visible trail.

Logan eyed the darkening sky. If their luck held, they'd find shelter before this hit. While he didn't mind rain, he sure as hell didn't want to be hit by lightning three days' ride outside of Pocatello. Not when everything else was going so well. There'd been no sign of the bounty hunter, no sign either that anyone had followed them into the mountains. Billy hadn't had any trouble; maybe the others had gotten away safely, too. Could it really be over?

He felt the first raindrops hit his face and finally began to hope.

"WHERE ARE WE?"

"Get inside!"

"But someone—"

"Get the hell inside, *now!*" He draped a saddlebag over her good shoulder. "Can you take the food?"

"Yes." She wouldn't have refused, though her arm was aching and she wanted to cry with exhaustion. Elizabeth bent her head against the wind and struggled to the cabin. Unlike the small miner's shack where they'd stayed after the robbery, this cabin looked well made and cared for. She knocked on the door.

"Hello!" she cried over the wind and the pelting rain. She was drenched from head to toe, despite the coat she was wearing. They'd ridden for an eternity while the rain beat down. Now she understood the biggest advantage of the cowboy hat. The wide brim kept the rain off her face and the back of her neck.

The cabin was dark and silent, but Elizabeth still hated opening the log door without being invited. There was enough light left in the afternoon to see that the large room was tidy and held furniture built from logs and homemade pegs. With no windows cut into the logs, the room had an intimate, cavelike feeling. She bent over and dumped the saddlebag on the floor, then found a lantern, lit it and set it on the crude table near the center of the room. A thick layer of dust coated everything, but there was a wood-burning cookstove and what looked like a real mattress on a rough-hewn bed. Whoever lived here had enjoyed his comforts.

Elizabeth opened the bottom of the stove to see if nthere was any wood ready to burn, but the holder was empty. A stack of firewood lay in the corner, though, so she imitated what she had seen Bob do back in Devil's Slide and then lit the kindling. No matter how tired she was, they would still need a fire. She was chilled clear through and knew that Logan would be drenched after taking care of the horses. He'd taken them to a small shed attached to the cabin.

Logan threw the door open and staggered in with the rest of the saddlebags and supplies. He kicked the door shut behind him and tossed the bags on the floor next to Elizabeth's before looking around the room.

"No one here?"

"No. Do you think it's all right if we stay here?"

He stared at her as if she'd lost her mind. "You'd rather sleep out in the rain tonight?"

"I don't want to get shot for trespassing."

Logan stepped over to the table and blew a layer of dust from its surface. "I don't think trespassing is a problem."

"Who do you think owns it? And why would they leave?"

"The Cramer brothers told me these mountains are full of old cabins. Men have been trapping and hunting these parts for years. We've been damn lucky so far." Logan stepped closer to the stove. "Hey, you got a fire going."

She nodded. "I watched Bob often enough to figure I could do it myself."

"Good." He examined the woodpile. "There's more out in the shed where I put the horses. We'll be warm enough."

Elizabeth shivered. "I hope you're right. I'm wet clear through."

He frowned. "You don't want to catch the fever again. Get into some dry clothes."

"I can't."

"Why not?" At the look on her face, he realized what the problem was. "Look, I'm not going back out in that storm, either. I'll just turn my back and you do what you have to do."

"It's not that. I don't have any other clothes. You tore up my petticoat and burned my blue dress. All I have is what I'm wearing. You even made me leave my nightgown back at the hotel."

"Then wrap yourself up in one of the blankets." He looked down at her, exasperated, as she shrugged off the large coat and draped it over the lone chair. "That's what I'm going to do as soon as it warms up in here."

Her eyebrows raised, but she didn't say anything. Logan stood by the stove and took the lifter that hung from the wall. He lifted the front round burner and checked the fire, then added more wood through the bottom door. He ignored Elizabeth as she opened the bedrolls and spread the damp blankets over the table to dry.

Without saying a word, she used her good arm to drag the heavy saddlebags across the floor. Logan stopped her, picking up the one with his money and tossing it over by the bed. "I don't want that too close to the fire," he said. He picked up the others and unpacked the supplies. He found the licorice he'd bought yesterday and turned to give it to her, but Elizabeth was busy unbuttoning her shirt and didn't notice that he'd turned to face her.

He knew it was wrong, but he watched her fiddle with the buttons. She'd taken her arm from the sling and was carefully using her right hand along with her left. She was frowning, though he remembered she'd managed to remove part of her shirt with no trouble this morning.

He crossed the room in two long strides and stood in front of her. "Here," he said, his voice softer than he'd intended. "Let me help you."

"I can do it," she insisted, but she stopped working the buttons.

"Why don't you just pull it over your head?"

"I tried," she said, "but I can't get the sleeve past the bandage this time, and my arm's sore."

"Sit down." He nudged her toward the bed and crouched so that he was at eye level. He finished unbuttoning the shirt. He told himself that his fingers were shaking because he was still cold from the spring rain and, when the pieces of fabric separated to reveal the chemise, he closed his eyes for a brief second and prayed for restraint. She shook her left arm from the sleeve, which made it easier to ease the fabric over the bandaged arm. When she shivered, he stopped and brought over a blanket for her shoulders.

Then he carefully eased the sleeve down her arm and assessed the bandage. No blood marred the cotton, but Logan untied it and unwrapped her arm.

"That feels better," she said, taking a deep breath. He realized how pale her skin had gone, and those blue eyes were clouded with pain once again. He hated that, knew it was all his fault.

"Maybe it should get some air."

"Maybe," she agreed. "I wish I knew more about medicine."

"What *do* you know about?"

She laughed, and the sound went right to his heart and eased the block of worry that had settled in his chest. "Not much that's going to help me out here. I organize people and take care of problems and design work strategies. I was in the process of getting my master's degree in management."

"You went to college?"

"Yes. It wasn't easy. I worked days and took courses at night."

"You must be a very smart woman." He wanted to tell her how beautiful she was, but he had no way to say the words without sounding false.

She shrugged, and the blanket slipped off her shoulder. He reached without thinking and tugged it back over her bare skin. But he didn't move his hand from her shoulder where her hair lay damp and waving along her neck. Instead, he reached up and cupped the back of her neck and brought her to him. She didn't resist when he moved both his hands to her neck to tangle in her hair. He brushed her lips with his and knew he had to kiss her, that he wouldn't stop kissing her easily.

This was madness. Touching this woman was foolish. But he could no more keep his mouth from hers than he could stop the rain from pounding on the cabin roof. He kissed her lips softly at first, afraid somehow he would hurt her. She gripped his shoulder with her left hand, and her lips parted beneath his. He was on fire. He dragged his mouth lower, to her cheek and the slender column of her throat, to taste rain on her skin. He took her lips again and urged her closer, and she inhaled sharply and cried out.

He stopped and lifted his mouth from hers. "Lizzie?"

"My arm," she said.

"I'm sorry," he managed to say. He'd inadvertently touched her arm, though he'd tried so hard to be gentle. Logan released her and Elizabeth leaned away from him.

"It's okay. It just hurt for a minute."

He remained crouched in front of her and kept his hands tight on his knees. He wanted to take her in his arms and feel a woman nestled against his chest once again. He struggled to remember what they had been talking about and took a deep breath. "You were talking about college. What about your family? Didn't they approve of a woman getting educated?"

"They weren't much help." Elizabeth's voice shook. She tugged the blanket across her chest again. "What about yours? Billy said you used to live in California?"

"Yeah." He let her change the subject, but he didn't forget the way she'd avoided giving him a direct answer. "My father is dead and my mother lives back in Kansas with one of her sisters. We farmed in the San Joaquin Valley." Logan stood. "I'll leave the bandage off for a while."

"Okay. I'm going to get out of the rest of these clothes."

Logan forced himself to walk away and fiddle with the stove. He didn't ask if she needed help. He hoped like hell she wouldn't. He didn't know how much more he could take. She was beautiful and courageous, even if she did expect him to believe her strange story. He wouldn't add rape to his long list of sins, though seduction was a definite consideration.

And the last thing he needed to continue. He would keep his hands off her from now on. He would not touch her or kiss her, no matter the enticing color of her eyes or the way her skin turned shades of rose from the campfire at night.

Logan grabbed his coat and the canteens and went outside, leaving Elizabeth to remove her clothing in privacy. Lightning seemed the lesser of two evils, he decided, clapping his hat on his head.

SHE WRAPPED the blanket around her as tightly as she could and held her pantalets and chemise over the stove. Heat blasted from the cookstove, making Elizabeth's cheeks grow red as she stood there. After Logan left, she'd quickly stripped off her underthings so she could dry them in private. Logan had looked edgy, as if he had something worrying him.

Well, he could make a list and take his pick, she supposed. Having your face on a wanted poster and carrying around forty thousand dollars in cash would be two things to lose sleep over. He didn't look like a man who would get upset over a kiss.

Although it had felt more like foreplay. He touched her and she melted, which was a dangerous reaction. Maybe it was because they'd been together for so many days. Alone together, day in and day out.

Maybe she was attracted to him because he had taken care of her. Or because his strength was something she'd come to rely upon. Elizabeth didn't know what the attraction was, only that an attraction existed. And she didn't think she was the only one suffering from it, either.

She had to remind herself that she was alone in a cabin with an outlaw, a man who was trying to outrun the law. A man who had committed God only knew how many crimes. And yet she liked him and trusted him.

She more than liked him, she realized. But she was engaged to be married to a wonderful man who was respected and admired by his friends and family. A pillar of the community, a leader in the city, a man of high moral character. She didn't think that John would last two days out here in Utah.

And neither he nor his mother would approve of her staying with an outlaw, a man who had kidnapped her from her hotel room at gunpoint and taken her to watch a train robbery.

Her getting shot wasn't Logan's fault. Her damn horse hadn't liked the sound of dynamite, but she didn't know how she'd explain that to Evelyn Lovell. She didn't think she'd try.

The less said the better, Elizabeth decided. She would say she was kidnapped, blindfolded and forced up to the mountains. Or she could say she was hit on the head and had amnesia.

Getting back to Boston was the main priority. She could figure out the rest later. But she knew John would never accept the truth. There was no room in his well-ordered world for time travel and vibrating books.

Elizabeth realized her arm was getting too warm, so she hung the chemise on a nearby nail on the wall above the stove and continued to wave her underwear over the heat, though she had to back up a few inches. Logan would be back eventually, and she wanted to have her underwear on when he returned. That would be best for both of them.

She tried not to think of the other two times he'd kissed her. She tried not to think about the way his mouth slanted over hers and the heat that had spread alarmingly fast through her body from the touch of his hands.

Suddenly, the door opened, and a blast of rain followed Logan into the room. He was dripping wet, but he carried the canteens over his shoulder and an old bucket in one hand. "I knew I could find water," he said, setting the bucket down and kicking the door shut behind him. Then he turned and dropped the wooden bar in place, sealing the cabin from the wind and rain.

Elizabeth gripped her blanket tighter and bundled the damp underwear in her hand. How was she going to put on her underwear with him standing there? He stripped off his coat and hat and came to stand beside her at the stove. He rubbed his hands over the heat and looked at the chemise, then at the bundle of white in her hand.

"I'd guess I came back too soon," he drawled.

"I'd say so," she agreed. There was no sense being modest, especially since she was not about to put on damp underwear. Elizabeth shook the pantelets and, careful to hold the blanket in place as best she could, hung them on the hook along with the chemise.

Logan moved over to the chair and sat down. He pulled off his boots and socks, then unbuttoned his shirt. "You'll have to excuse me," he told her, his gray eyes twinkling as she quickly moved away from the stove.

"I'll get you a blanket," Elizabeth offered, hurrying to unroll the bedding piled near the bed. "You'd better get all those wet clothes off."

"Then you'd better turn around."

Elizabeth dumped the blanket on the table and went over to the bed. She couldn't resist lying down on the mattress and, facing the wall, she curled the blanket securely around her. She was asleep within minutes, dreaming of Boston and her wedding day. She was wearing a long white beaded dress, and when she walked down the aisle, there was a revolver strapped to her hip.

9

LOGAN WOKE with two soft breasts pressed against his naked chest and Elizabeth's head on his shoulder. He stared at those lovely breasts for a long minute, then forced himself to look away. The wound on her arm was an angry red, but didn't look as swollen as it had last night. The corner of her lips touched his skin and her eyes were closed. He blinked sleepily and looked back down at those breasts again. He lifted his hand to touch one, but stopped. He would only wake her up and there would be hell to pay.

God only knew what she'd think.

His body tightened and hardened and touched the smooth sweep of her thigh. Logan looked down and realized with a combination of ecstasy and horror that their bodies were touching lengthwise, from shoulder to toe, and he was hotter than he had been in years.

He should have been a gentleman and let her have the bed to herself last night, but he had longed to lie down on something other than the hard ground or wooden floor. Elizabeth had curled herself into a ball and was well over on one side of the bed. There'd been plenty of room for a man there in the remaining part of the mattress.

He suspected she wouldn't take kindly to sharing a bed with him. He figured she'd say that sleeping beside him on the floor or outside wasn't at all the same thing.

He was getting to know her pretty well. And he'd also known he wasn't going to sleep on something hard when he could sleep on something soft. The fact that Elizabeth was naked as a jaybird underneath that blanket was a fact he'd chosen to ignore.

But this morning, he sure couldn't ignore the soft body tangled with his, nor his reaction to it. She'd sought his warmth in the night before. He should have known she would do it again.

Almost afraid to breathe, Logan lay quietly in the semidarkness and let the sleeping woman rest on his shoulder. His arm was numb; he'd lost all feeling in his fingers. He didn't care. Delicate pink nipples touched his chest. He felt very big and very clumsy and terrified that she would waken and the moment would be over. He prayed for five minutes, then he prayed for an hour.

Then he began to pray she'd waken and he could stop torturing himself.

Elizabeth stirred and snuggled deeper against the comforting warm wall. Even half-asleep she was careful to keep her injured arm motionless. She was so very, very comfortable. She was in a bed, she realized. A lovely bed with blankets and...she was not alone. Slowly, she realized her skin was touching someone else's, and her eyes flew open to see Logan's silver-gray ones looking down at her with concern. And something else.

"What are you doing?" she whispered. She froze, afraid to move.

"Nothing," he replied. "I didn't want to sleep on the floor, and in the night you must have crawled closer to me. While you were sleeping." He didn't add that she did it all the time.

"But you're . . . naked."

"My clothes were wet," he explained, "just like yours. I wrapped myself in a blanket and went to sleep."

"Well, you're not asleep anymore." The evidence of just how awake he was lay against her thigh, and she blushed.

"I didn't want to wake you." He brushed a strand of hair from her face. "And I have to admit, I wasn't in any hurry to leave this bed."

Elizabeth tried to pull the blanket between them, but the material was stuck underneath her hip. She couldn't hope to budge it with her bad arm, so she tried to wriggle away from contact with Logan's hard body before she succumbed to the urge to run her palm along his furred chest. He was gorgeous, all tight muscle and smooth flesh. She was sleepy and warm and entirely too comfortable.

"Hell, Lizzie, I'm not going to rape you," Logan said. "Slide off my blanket and I'll get up."

He was squeezed between her body and the wall, she realized. She'd practically pinned him against the logs and draped herself over him. "I'm sorry," she murmured, flustered with her body's reaction to touching him. She was hot and shivery, curious and shy. She rolled over on her back and took as much of the blanket as she could to cover herself.

Logan winced as he moved his arm and flexed his fingers. "Hold still a minute," he said, and tried to climb over her to the far edge of the bed. The blanket caught and held him above her. His hip nudged hers, his body hung motionless against her. He looked down into her eyes and swore.

"Hell, Lizzie."

He brought his lips to hers and kissed her with the same searing passion she'd felt before whenever he touched her. Elizabeth felt as if her body was melting under his. It was insane to want him, crazy beyond belief to yearn to make love with him, but she wanted to feel his skin against hers. She wanted to go on kissing him, she wanted to know what it would feel like to have him inside of her.

She was crazy, she knew, but Elizabeth touched her fingertips to his bare shoulder and pulled him closer. He groaned into her mouth as she parted her lips and his tongue teased hers. He dropped lower, carefully taking the weight of his body onto his forearms as he covered her body with his. He lifted his head.

"Am I hurting you?"

"No," she whispered, smoothing her palm over his bearded cheek. Each day, he looked more disreputable. Each day, she was more attracted to him, more intrigued with him.

"Open your legs," he said, trailing his lips along her jawline. She kicked the blankets to one side, and Logan settled himself between her thighs. She inhaled as he moved over her most sensitive skin, but Logan stopped short of entering her. She was wet and slick and ready, and of course he was aware of that, but Elizabeth didn't want to wait.

His lips touched the tops of her breasts and sent another round of shivers throughout her skin. He was on top of her, he was heavy between her thighs. And yet she knew, if she wanted, she could stop him with one word.

"Beautiful," he murmured, touching his lips with hers. Then he looked down at her, his beautiful mouth frowning. "Am I going to hurt you?"

She knew what he was asking and shook her head. "No."

With that, he entered her, inch by agonizing inch, as if he wanted to make the sensation last. Each time, he pulled back, going deeper with each stroke, until he'd filled her. He was bigger than she imagined, bigger than she'd thought possible, and she closed her eyes as he moved within her. Inevitable, she thought, reaching for him, touching his mouth. There was a rightness to this act of lovemaking that stunned her. No guilt or shame, no embarrassment. Just the knowledge that this was the way making love was supposed to be.

He belonged here, within her. She belonged here, in his arms. His mouth came down on hers and heat centered on the joining of their bodies. Elizabeth forgot who she was and where she was; it ceased to matter as the exquisite sensations built inside her. He made love to her as if she was beautiful and fragile and desirable, as if he couldn't get enough. The tension built to an almost unbearable peak, then Elizabeth shattered around him. He thrust deeper still, until his own climax shook his body and he filled her with his hot seed.

Logan lifted his mouth from hers and kissed her neck as Elizabeth slowly came back to awareness. They were still joined together; Logan was still hard within her. Long minutes of silence passed as they kissed gently in the semidarkness of the room.

"It sounds like it's still raining," he said, a slight smile crossing his face.

She felt very vulnerable, still pinned to the mattress, and struggled to think of something to say. "Are we riding today?"

"We are not," he declared. "We're going to do this again." She smiled, and he kissed the corner of her mouth that turned up. "Then you agree?"

"We shouldn't be wasting time," Elizabeth said, knowing she would be content to spend weeks in this bed with Logan.

He looked down at her and pretended to be insulted. "'Wasting time', huh? That's what you call it?"

"I call it crazy," she answered, palming her hand along his muscled arm.

His expression grew serious. "I've wanted you since I first saw you," he said. "I've slept beside you every night and I've fought the urge to touch you, even though you'd snuggle up to me like a damn kitten. Yeah," he muttered, "It's crazy, all right." He moved his hips, sending tiny tremors of awareness through her body. "I'm so crazy, I'm afraid to leave you, for fear I'll never be inside you again."

"We can't stay like this," she whispered.

"We can't?" He thrust slowly, careful not to withdraw completely, but asserting his possession of her.

Elizabeth touched his lips with her fingertips. "I didn't expect this." She wished she could tell him how much he meant to her, but Elizabeth hesitated. She wasn't sure herself what all this meant, either, and as Logan moved within her, she wasn't sure she cared.

"Don't stop me, Lizzie."

"I don't want to."

He coaxed every sweet sensation from her body until a long while later, spent and trembling, she closed her eyes and slept.

ELIZABETH WOKE to the smell of meat cooking and sat up to see Logan standing at the cookstove, his back to her. He'd propped open the door for light and air, she realized, and a cool draft cleansed the stuffy cabin, though rain still pelted the ground. Logan was dressed, she noted, and the back of his hair looked wet. He'd probably been outside to take care of the horses while she was asleep.

She wanted to go to the bathroom. She was starving. And she wanted a hot bath. And in that order, too. She climbed off the bed and grabbed a blanket to cover herself with. Not that she had any secrets left after the past hours. She cringed inwardly. She was engaged to marry one man; she'd made love to another. She'd never done anything like that before. In fact, she'd prided herself on her common sense and good judgment.

Now she'd spent the morning making love to a handsome outlaw. And she hadn't given a thought to birth control or the transmission of sexual diseases. She was an idiot. A sexually satisfied idiot.

Logan turned around and watched her walk across the room. His face remained expressionless, as if he was waiting to see her reaction to him in the daylight.

Elizabeth had nothing to say. She stuck her feet in her boots and, clad in nothing but a blanket, headed outside for a few minutes of privacy. Logan handed her a cup of coffee when she returned, but neither spoke. He shoved a dish of bread and salted beef in front of her and didn't wait for her to thank him. Instead, he grabbed his hat and coat and left the cabin as if a thousand demons were chasing him.

Her heart sank. She should have said something, but talking about sex didn't come easy to her. John had been matter-of-fact about using a condom, although he'd had a vasectomy years ago. They'd had blood tests when they became engaged; they'd stopped using condoms six months later. There would be no children, of course. He'd made that clear. Anyway, she wasn't sure she would be a good mother. She certainly hadn't grown up with role models for "Mother of the Year."

She sipped her coffee and ate her breakfast and blinked back tears. She knew he wouldn't leave her. The saddlebags were pushed under the bed. Even when he was sleeping, he was protecting everything he had.

Just as he'd protected her. Elizabeth Richardson, loner and imposter, had finally depended on someone and that man was an outlaw, running from the law and almost certain to end up shot dead from a marshal's bullet.

Elizabeth leaned her head on her hands and groaned out loud. It was more than feeling protected. She was falling in love with him. She was twenty-six years old and she had fallen in love for the first time in her life—with the wrong man in the wrong century.

It was time to go home.

"WHAT ARE YOU DOING?" Logan paused in the doorway and watched Elizabeth shove clothing into a saddlebag. She was wearing one of his shirts and her legs were intriguingly bare. Since they were the same legs that had been wrapped around him earlier this morning, he looked at them longingly.

"Packing."

"Yeah, well, I can see that." He crossed his arms in front of his chest. "Where do you think you're going?"

"Boston."

"To that man you're marrying."

She didn't look at him. "Yes."

"Nearest train is three days' ride," he drawled. "You don't even know what direction."

"North," she declared. "I've been paying attention."

Logan strode over to her and crouched by her. "And what will you do for food, Lizzie?" He tugged a lock of her hair so she would face him. There was a look of near panic in those blue eyes that unnerved him. He kept his voice soft as he asked, "What will you do without me?"

Tears welled in her eyes as she gazed up at him. "I don't know," she whispered. "That's the problem."

He opened his arms and held her. "I promised to take you to the train, Lizzie. I keep my promises, though you don't know me well enough to know that. I'm a man of my word."

"I know," she said.

He lifted her in his arms and walked over to the bed. Logan sat down, cradling the woman on his lap. "You love this Boston man?"

There was silence, and Logan held his breath waiting to hear her reply.

"Yes. No. I don't know," she admitted. "I mean, it's not like . . . that."

"Why are you marrying him then?"

This time, she didn't answer, though Logan waited in the silence and listened to the wind sweep through the treetops. The worst of the storm had passed, but the rain continued. They could leave now, but his heart wasn't in it. Because Elizabeth wanted to leave, he found himself determined to stay here one more day. One day's rest wouldn't hurt the horses. One day's rest would be good for all of them.

Logan spoke into the silence. "I brought a bucket of water from the creek in case you want a bath."

Elizabeth tilted her head toward him and smiled. "I'd like that."

Encouraged, Logan grinned back. "Guess that means you changed your mind about leaving."

"I can wait a few more days if I have to." Her gaze dropped down to his mouth, and Logan, unable to stop himself, bent lower and captured her lips. He kissed her until they were both breathless and sprawled on the mattress, then he helped her off the bed before he could make love to her again.

"Come on," he said, tugging her toward the stove. "I'll teach you how to heat up water."

"What about you?"

"I bathed in the creek," he said. "Colder than hell out there, too."

She shook her head. "You're a tough man, Logan."

He bent over and poured water into a black kettle. "I haven't had any other choice."

SHE WAS WEARING dry clothes and a stew was simmering on the stove. Her hair was wet, but fairly clean. Logan had helped her wash and rinse it and, though he had touched her as little as possible in the process, she'd managed to disguise the unsettling effect he had on her. She'd combed through the wet strands with her fingers until the tangles disappeared, while Logan went outside while she dressed in yesterday's clothes.

They both studiously avoided looking at the bed. It was best, Elizabeth decided, that they keep their minds off what had taken place this morning.

That was an accident, she realized, a lapse in judgment that shouldn't happen again.

Logan brought the lantern to the table and sat down. Then he spread a deck of cards across the rough boards. "Do you play poker?"

"A few times, when I was a kid. It's been a long time."

"It'll come back to you."

She sat down across from him. "What are we going to bet with?"

He smiled. "There's forty thousand dollars under the bed."

"That's yours." She remembered the robbery. "Sort of."

"Oh, it's mine, all right," he assured her, sweeping the cards into a neat stack.

"You really believe that, don't you?"

"The Southern Pacific took my land. *Stole* my land, my father's land. I just stole enough back to start over again." He shuffled the cards and placed the deck in front of her. "Cut."

She did, and slid the deck of cards back to him.

He stood up and retrieved the saddlebag with the money in it, then brought a stack of bills to the table. He split them in half and slid a pile of money to her side of the table. "Call it a loan."

Elizabeth gulped. She'd never been much of a card-player. "I don't know much about poker."

"I'll teach you." He put a bill in the center of the table and motioned for Elizabeth to do likewise. Then he dealt them each five cards, and told her to pick up her cards. "One pair of anything is fine. A straight is when all the numbers are consecutive, like deuce, three, four, five and six. A flush is when the cards are all the same suit."

"Okay." Elizabeth studied her hand. One ace, a pair of sixes and a ten and a five. At least she had a pair.

Logan tossed another hundred-dollar bill into the pile. "Dealer opens. Are you in?"

"Okay." She put in another bill. "Now I get to throw some away, right?"

He nodded. "Yeah. It's five card draw. How many do you want?"

"Two." She put the ten and the five facedown off to one side, then Logan dealt her two cards. She watched as he discarded three cards and dealt himself three more before she looked at her hand. Another ace and a six. So she had two pair. She didn't think it was that great a poker hand, although it would beat one pair of anything.

"It's your bet," Logan said, so Elizabeth placed another bill on the pile. Logan studied his cards, then tossed in money of his own. "Call," he said. "That means you have to show me your cards. I just paid for the privilege."

She laid down her hand. "Two pair."

His eyebrows rose. "You win."

She scooped the money toward her. "You don't have to sound so surprised."

"Beginner's luck," he muttered, but his eyes twinkled as he gathered up the cards and handed her the deck to shuffle. "Your deal, lady."

They'd played for hours, until light no longer filtered through the spaces between the logs and Logan had refilled the stove with wood twice. They ate more stew and opened the last bottle of whiskey to warm them from the dampness. Elizabeth relaxed, and they both pretended they hadn't made love that morning. Gradually, Elizabeth lost her winnings, until she was completely out of money.

"I'm done," she announced, throwing down another losing hand. "I've lost all the money you owed me. Easy come, easy go."

"You're not much of a cardplayer." He shook his head. "You're just not serious enough."

She grinned. Drinking whiskey abolished every serious bone in her body. "And you are?"

"I try." He leaned back and stretched. "Guess they still play poker in . . . 1996, is it?"

"Yes. People still play cards, like gin rummy and bridge and hearts and poker. But there are lots of other things to do. We have television and video games and—"

"What the hell is all that?"

"You can watch shows on a little screen in a box." He stared at her, and she added, "Don't ask me to explain computers and Super Nintendo."

He handed her the bottle. "All right. I won't."

"I got in big trouble playing poker once," Elizabeth mused out loud. "At St. Mary's—at the place where I went to school—some of the older girls dared us to play strip poker. My roommate and I were in seventh grade and didn't know how to play, but we didn't want to act like we were afraid, so we did it on a dare. The housemother caught us before we were stark naked." She took a sip of whiskey and giggled. "I'll never forget the look on her face."

He grinned and pushed the cards to her. "I've never played strip poker before."

"And you're not going to now."

Logan put his money in a deliberate stack. "Seems to me you're going to need money to get back to Boston."

Elizabeth laughed. "Are you serious?"

His smile told her he wasn't, but there was a gleam
in his eyes that made her skin tingle with awareness that
she was here, alone, with a man she was probably falling in love with, and she'd just been dared to a game of
strip poker.

There were worse ways to spend an evening. She took
another swallow of whiskey, then handed the bottle
back to him. "Don't give me any more of that. I have
to keep my wits about me and my clothes on."

Logan shuffled the cards. "You lose the game, you
take off your clothes."

"Uh-uh. I lose, I take off one piece of clothing. I win,
I win five hundred dollars."

"One hundred."

"Three hundred."

"One hundred," he repeated. "I worked hard for this
money and there isn't any more where that came from."

"Well, all right."

He nodded. "You get a pile of money, you have your
choice to forfeit the money."

Elizabeth considered the question. She could remove a piece of clothing or pay one hundred dollars.
That was reasonable, she figured, though her brain was
a little foggy from the liquor. "If we were playing this
the right way, you'd have to take off your clothes when
you lost a round, but I'd rather have your money."

"I'll take that as a comment on how much you need
money," he drawled, "and not as a slur on my appearance."

"I don't think you need to worry about your looks,"
she replied, gathering up her cards. "You'd be a big hit
in Boston, even with the beard."

He started to pick up his cards and stopped. "What's
wrong with my beard?"

"You looked better in Salt Lake, when you just had that day-old growth. The scruffy look is 'in,' by the way."

Logan gave a disgusted sigh and picked up his cards. He grinned. "Do I get to pick what comes off first?"

"Not on your life." Elizabeth knew the boots and the socks would count as four, her shirt as five, pants as six, and by that time she would have won enough to quit. Even if she only won half the time, she would still win enough money for some new clothes and her hotel room. Logan had said he'd give her the ticket, after all. Once she'd acquired five hundred dollars, she would quit. Logan was too much of a gentleman to insist she keep playing after she didn't want to. Heck, if she was on a winning streak, she'd play him for sole possession of the bed.

Two hours later, Elizabeth's boots lay, along with her socks, on the rough floor underneath the table. She eyed her last hundred-dollar bill and then considered the cards in her hand. Three queens. The best hand she'd had for what seemed like an eternity.

"You sleeping or playing?" Logan looked pleased with himself. Too pleased, she worried. Or was he bluffing? She laid her cards on the table and waited for his reaction. He put his down, revealing a royal flush. "That beats three queens," he announced. "Now what?"

Elizabeth wanted to keep that hundred dollars. She also wanted to keep her pants on. "Guess the shirt goes," she said, with more bravado than she felt. What had seemed like a great way to make money now seemed totally ridiculous. She unbuttoned the baggy shirt and tossed it aside. Clad only in her chemise, she took the cards and began to shuffle. She told herself that the chemise covered as much of her as the white silk tank top did, underneath her navy suit, but she still felt more exposed than she wanted to be. But what the hell, she figured. No one in Boston would ever know. Once she returned to Salt Lake, she'd be in that hotel room and out of that hotel room before you could say "cosmic door."

Logan shook his head. "You're a dangerous woman when you've been drinking whiskey, Lizzie."

"I'm not much of a drinker, and my luck has to turn sometime." She watched while he cut the cards, then she dealt the next hand.

"You sure about that?" Logan studied the cards he'd been dealt.

"It's the law of averages." Four, seven, five, six and a jack. She could draw a three or an eight and have a straight.

"I don't know much about that, but I do know that some nights it's better to quit while you're ahead." He tossed a bill into the middle of the table. "I think in the morning, when your head clears, you're going to regret this."

"I'm willing to take the chance. How many cards do you want?"

"One," he said, discarding a card with the flick of a wrist as Elizabeth dealt him a new one.

"Me, too." She tossed the jack aside and dealt herself another card. She added it to the cards in her hand and then looked to see what it was. Her heart raced with excitement when she saw the three of hearts. She was going to win this one. She could feel it. Elizabeth kept her face expressionless. "How about doubling up?"

Logan didn't blink. He tossed another bill onto the table. "And I pick the second piece of clothing."

She nodded and placed her cards on the table. "Read 'em and weep. I finally got a straight."

The outlaw placed his cards with hers. "Straight, queen high."

"What does that mean?"

"I win," he declared. "Your high card is an eight. Mine's a queen."

Elizabeth reached for the whiskey bottle, but Logan moved it away from her. "No more," he said, his eyes glinting silver in the light of the lantern. "You've had enough whiskey for one night. You're unlucky enough without being drunk, too."

"I'm not drunk."

"You will be, if you keep going like this."

"I'm a little...tipsy," she admitted. She stood up and began to unfasten her pants. Logan watched as the fabric dropped to the floor and she kicked it away. There was something to be said for striptease, Elizabeth decided. There was a power in it she hadn't realized, a power to entice a man and hold his attention. Still, she couldn't believe she was standing before Logan in a chemise and knee-length cotton drawers. She cleared her throat and his gaze met hers. "You get to choose, remember?"

"The top," he growled.

Elizabeth unbuttoned the top button with shaking fingers, then progressed slowly down the front of the chemise until the fabric separated in two. She held it together until, taking a deep breath, she began to move it from her shoulders.

"Damn it, take the money!" Logan stood up and shoved hundreds of dollars onto the floor. "You don't have to act like a whore." He glared at her as he stepped closer. "I won't have that on my conscience along with everything else I've done."

"Your conscience?" she echoed.

He reached for her then, and hurriedly tried to refasten the tiny buttons. He made a clumsy job of it, and the second his fingers touched her bare skin, Elizabeth knew she was lost.

10

IT WAS MADNESS to touch the buttons of her chemise when all Logan wanted to do was place his lips against the sweet cleft between her breasts.

His fingers stilled in their struggles to button together the pieces of fabric. Pure unadulterated lust filled him, making him lose all sense of time and place. Logan could only feel the smooth skin under his fingertips, and when he parted the cotton, it was to rub his palms along Elizabeth's full breasts.

He looked into her face, watched her blue eyes darken, felt her nipples harden under his hands. She wanted him, and the knowledge filled him with power, power to use in pleasuring her.

"I think I have lost, after all," he groaned.

Elizabeth smiled. "Ask yourself, Mr. Younger," she drawled. "Do you feel lucky today?"

"Yes," he said, chuckling. His anger at himself dissipated, and he was left with that odd sensation of rightness. "I feel very lucky today."

He swept the clothing from her shoulders, carefully easing the fabric past the bandage. She stood there, naked from the waist up, beautiful in the light of the lantern. He'd always thought she was beautiful. Logan couldn't believe that she was his, at least for now. He slid his hands to her waist to prevent her from moving.

He kissed her then, taking her mouth with a force that nearly knocked them both to the floor. Logan gripped her waist to keep her from falling, then kissed her until there was no breath left. When he finally lifted his mouth, her lips were swollen and moist.

"You make me crazy. I don't care where you're from," he murmured, gazing into her eyes. "Whatever the story, it makes no difference. Not now. Not here."

"No," Elizabeth agreed breathlessly. "Not now."

He lifted her in his arms and placed her carefully on the bed. "Your arm—"

"Doesn't hurt," she said, filling in his sentence for him. "I must be a quick healer."

"You're tough," he answered. "I can't believe just how tough you are."

"I don't feel that way." She felt soft and feminine and desirable. She watched him turn off the lantern, plunging the room into inky darkness. She listened to the rustle of his clothing, the creaking of the mattress as he sat on the bed, the clunk of his boots as they hit the floor one at a time. Logan turned and stretched out on his side to face her and hooked one long leg over both of hers to hold her against him.

"So you don't disappear," he whispered into her ear.

A delicious feeling of being wanted swept over her. She didn't care that it was only for one day, one night. Somehow, that didn't matter. When he lowered his mouth to hers, she knew he wanted her, desired her, in a way she'd never experienced before. "I'm not going anywhere."

"You might." He swept his hand through her hair and rubbed her neck. "You appeared like magic. You could leave the same way."

"I wish it was that easy."

His voice was teasing as his lips caressed her cheek. "You want to leave me that badly, then?"

Elizabeth couldn't reply. She lay in a naked tangle with one man while engaged to marry another. And worse, she no longer could feel guilty about it. She wanted this man.

She was falling in love with him.

"Lizzie?"

She touched his face, brushed the palm of her hand across his beard. "You're very handsome without this."

"I'll shave once we get to Pocatello," he promised. "Before you leave."

"I don't want to talk about leaving." His erection was hard against her thigh, making thought difficult.

"All right," he agreed, his voice low. He kissed her slowly, easing his tongue between her parted lips and sweeping his hand to her breast. He released her legs and nudged her onto her back, then kissed a hot trail down her body. He took one beaded nipple into his mouth and suckled, gently at first and then with increasing pressure until heat pulsated through her body and centered between her thighs.

His fingers found the slick wetness there and, stroking slowly, made Elizabeth dizzy with desire. She was on fire as he moved lower, and ran his lips over her abdomen. The soft beard grazed the tender skin and sent shivers through her. His lips found her, his tongue laved sensitive flesh while his fingers teased and probed until Elizabeth thought the world had spun out of control.

Logan sensed when she was on the edge of release, and he slowly withdrew. He slid his body over hers and fit himself inside her with excruciating slowness until, knowing he was no longer able to control his passion, he moved inside her fully. Penetrating and withdrawing within that tight canal was an ecstasy he thought he'd never know again. She met him, took him deep with every thrust, pulled him into her with an answering need. He grit his teeth and pleasured the woman beneath him until she moaned and tightened around him. His own dizzying release followed quickly upon hers and he cried out as he thrust into her.

Logan dropped slowly into her welcoming arms and waited for his battered heart to stop pounding against his rib cage. He could still taste her on his lips. He wanted to taste her again. God help him, he never wanted to let her go.

"TELL ME about the future."

"What do you want to know?"

Logan kissed her shoulder and rolled over onto his back. "Tell me how you make love in 1996."

Elizabeth leaned on her elbow and, trying not to laugh, looked down at him. Her eyes had adjusted to the darkness and she could make out the planes of his face. "We made love four times today, Logan. Did you notice any difference?"

"Can't say as I did," he drawled.

"I don't know if that's a good thing or not," she said.

"Oh, it was different, all right," he said. "Damn near killed me."

He took her by the waist, lifted her on top of him. She settled herself between his legs and propped herself up on one elbow. "I wouldn't want anything to happen to you," she teased.

He smoothed her hair from her forehead. "Nothing's going to happen to me," he said, his voice serious. "Not now."

"You're a wanted man."

He smiled. "Yeah. I've heard."

She rested her cheek on his chest while he stroked her back in smooth motions. "I wish you could come back with me. You'd be safe."

"I'm safe now."

"You're never safe," she murmured. "But you probably wouldn't like my world, either. Millions of people, cars, television, radio, space satellites, disease, pollution and war. It's not quiet, like this."

"And the good things?"

Elizabeth closed her eyes and thought for a minute. "Modern medicine. Penicillin. Birth control pills. Car phones, computers, e-mail and Ben and Jerry's ice cream."

"And the man you're going to marry," Logan added.

"Yes."

"Will you tell him about this?"

"I don't know." Elizabeth thought about all the times she'd lied to John about her family and her past, her antiques and her pictures. What was one more lie? The thought shamed her. "As far as he knows, I've disappeared. They probably think I've been kidnapped."

"You have," he told her. "I took you right out of the hotel. And now look where you are."

Elizabeth lifted her head and smiled at him. "Do you really want to know about sex in the nineties?"

"You're right quick to change the subject."

She ignored his comment and slid down his body to the semirigid arousal between his legs.

Logan propped himself on his elbows to watch her. "Lizzie, what in hell—"

She touched its smooth rounded tip, then cupped her hand around him. She looked up. "Do you want me to stop?"

He groaned, threw his head back and swore. Which, she assumed, meant he didn't want her to stop touching him. He felt like hard satin as he swelled in her hand. She wrapped her fingers around him and brought her lips to the tip of his hard flesh. She heard him groan again, and tentatively took him in her mouth. It was an act she had avoided until now, an act she'd found no pleasure in trying, but with Logan she wanted to taste him, wanted to take him into her mouth and feel that soft flesh against her tongue. She wanted to give him the pleasure he'd given her.

She wanted to make love to him, in every way possible. Because there was no future, of that she was certain. There would be no other days or nights after she reached the train. She would be alone again, with or without John.

Because she didn't love the man in Boston.

And never would.

He brought her up to him and entered her with a smooth stroke. His fingers gripped her buttocks as he thrust within her, bringing her to a swift climax before finding his own. She felt him pulse inside her and her own tremors still continued, slowly changing to contented bliss. Elizabeth brushed her cheek against Logan's warm chest. Now she knew what passion was. Now she knew what it was like to be loved.

LOGAN LAY in the dark and listened to Elizabeth's light, rhythmic breathing beside him. She was curled against him, of course, but this time it was intentional. This time, she'd nestled into his arms when she was awake. This time, he'd held her and not been afraid that she would waken in shock and fear.

He would love her again in the dawn, before they packed up and headed north once more. Two more nights on the trail and then Pocatello. He was so close. So very close. The beautiful woman with the blue eyes could get him killed. Hell, buying supplies almost got him killed. At least he'd known a woman's sweet loving again.

And she would be leaving. Logan slipped out of bed and rustled through the saddlebags until he found what he wanted. He held the book carefully, as if it would explode in his hand, and walked over to the cookstove. He could burn it. She would never know.

If he destroyed the book she believed would take her from him, Elizabeth couldn't leave. And he could keep her with him, go to Montana. Start over.

Logan opened the bottom door and hesitated. The damn book was her only possession. He'd taken what little else she had, including her freedom, and given her pain and hardship. Pain and hardship were what he'd given Sarah, too.

She'd paid with her life, but Elizabeth didn't have to. Logan tossed the book on the table, added several pieces of wood to the fire and went back to lie beside the sleeping woman who trusted him.

"ARE WE STILL in danger?" Elizabeth looked around at the thick forest. The pine needles still dripped moisture onto her hat and shoulders. They had been riding all day, much to her discomfort. Making love all night and then getting on a horse the next morning was not a combination she'd recommend to her girlfriends.

Logan turned and looked at her over his shoulder. "It's possible. It's always possible."

"That's not what I want to hear. You're supposed to say, 'Of course not,'" she grumbled.

"Of course not," he repeated, looking pleased to oblige her. "How's that?"

Elizabeth eyed the darkening sky. "Can we stop now?"

"Soon."

"Thank God," she muttered under her breath.

"I thought you wanted to get to Pocatello as soon as possible."

"I do. I just want to be alive when I get there." She should have known he'd hear her. He heard everything, saw everything, and it was getting on her nerves. She was so tired that everything, even the hawk circling overhead, was getting on her nerves. Her arm had just begun to ache and she longed to lie down by a fire and fall asleep in Logan's arms.

"That's my plan, too, Lizzie," he drawled. "We've been lucky so far. Damn lucky."

Elizabeth considered his words as she followed him along the wooded ridge. Every once in a while, she'd catch a glimpse of distant mountains, majestic and forbidding. The panoramas that Logan seemed to take for granted took her breath away with their magnificence. The West was enormous, with forests and mountains and rivers that seemed to go on forever. Lucky? Oh, yes. She was lucky to have seen all this, lucky to have her fate mixed up with Logan's, at least for a short while.

She'd learned about passion. She'd learned about love. Butch Cassidy had loved his schoolteacher, Etta, with a passion that had changed both their lives. Now she knew what that was like. And she would never forget what she'd known, long after she'd returned to

Boston and become Mrs. John Lovell and presided over the Beacon Street house.

Could she do that if she was in love with Logan Younger? Would she add another lie to all the lies she'd told already?

There was no question that she would return. The book had traveled to the past with her for a reason. While it could be an accident that she'd fallen through time, it was no accident that *Rogues Across Time* came with her, like a passport. A key to allow her to go back to the life she'd had before.

Yes, she wanted to reach Pocatello. She wanted to board the train to Salt Lake and stay in that particular hotel room once again.

But she didn't mind waiting a few more days. There would be much to face when she returned, and for now she was content to make her way through the mountains with Logan leading the way.

"STIR THIS," Logan said. He quickly made the biscuit dough and shaped it into smooth, flat rounds. "I sure wish you knew how to cook."

"I wish you'd quit saying that. It would be like me saying, 'I wish you had your driver's license.' And besides, you can't knead biscuits with one hand," Elizabeth replied.

"You're healing fast." He placed the biscuits on top of the sizzling strips of salted beef and Elizabeth took the wooden spoon from the pot.

"I'm getting used to your cooking."

"When I reach Montana—" Logan didn't finish the sentence. He clamped his lips together and put the lid on the cast-iron cooking pot.

"Montana? Is that where you're going next?"

He sighed. "Yeah. I'm buying a ranch and settling down. I would appreciate your keeping that information to yourself."

"I wouldn't tell anyone. What about the bounty hunter?"

"Richardson? That bastard will have to go after someone else. He knows I'll kill him if I ever see him, so he stays out of sight. Like a rattler curled up behind a rock."

The sudden violence in his voice surprised her. "You'd kill him if he tried to arrest you?"

"He was one of the guns that the railroad hired to get me off my land. The only reason I haven't done it before is 'cause I haven't had the opportunity."

"Have you—" She broke off, but then went ahead. "Killed a lot of men?"

His gray-eyed gaze held hers. "Do you really want to know?"

She nodded.

"Three," he replied. "All in self-defense. Two deaths I paid for, doing time in the prison at Santa Clara. The other was an outlaw who wanted my money and held a gun to Billy's head."

"Who did you go to prison for killing?"

"They were men from the railroad and their hired guns, trying to take my land and my father's land. The farmers in the county got together to fight them. There were a lot of men who died in the fields that day. And a ricochet bullet killed my wife."

"I'm sorry," Elizabeth whispered.

"My wife was dead and my land was gone. My father's heart failed after the shooting. He dropped dead right there in the fields. And the Southern Pacific won, anyway. The courts upheld their right to the land, despite the promises they'd made to the settlers who'd spent their lives farming it. The farmers went to prison and the railroad made more money."

"Bob told me once that you were all farmers."

"Yeah. A lifetime ago, in the San Joaquin Valley. I told you I was getting even with the railroad. Now I'm finished."

"The end justifies the means," she murmured. "I guess it does in this case."

"You have her eyes."

"Your wife's?"

His voice grew soft with memory. "They were blue, like yours."

"Tell me about her."

Logan didn't answer right away. He seemed to be remembering, and the tight lines around his mouth softened when he finally responded. "I knew her all my life. She was the preacher's middle daughter. She had yellow hair and blue eyes and a smile that made a man think of sunshine in January. She didn't approve of fighting the railroad. She wanted to leave, find somewhere else and start over, but I had my pride." He shook his head. "I still have my pride and nothing else," he repeated, his voice bitter. "And she's dead and buried."

"You must have loved her very much." She wished she could comfort him, but she was afraid to move toward him. Finally, she mustered the courage to move to his side, on the other side of the fire. She tucked her arm under his and leaned her head on his shoulder, then they both watched the small flames crackle around the coals for a long time.

"I've heard Montana is beautiful," Elizabeth said. "Why did you pick it?"

"Because it's far away from here," he explained. "I've robbed a lot of trains from Sacramento to Ogden. I can't go back to California and no one expects me to go north. They'll figure I'll head south and keep stealing from the railroad."

"Instead, you'll disappear and live happily ever after, to the ripe old age of ninety-five." She prayed the words were true.

"Yeah. I'm going to be a dull old man who will tell stories of the old days that no one will believe." He put his arm around her and held her close to him.

"I'll find out what happened, you know. I can go through old records and see where you settled and how long you lived."

"That's an odd thing to consider. I'll be walking around in one century when you're in another. In one I'm alive and in the other I'm dead." He shook his head. "Hard to get used to, I'll say that."

"You believe me?"

"I don't know what to believe. That's the honest truth, too."

"I've told a lot of lies in my life," Elizabeth admitted, "but this isn't one of them."

"What kind of lies could you tell?" His eyes sparkled with amusement.

"All sorts," she admitted. "About my past. Who I am and where I came from, but this is the truth, Logan. I wouldn't lie about something like this."

"I appreciate that." He poked the fire and the flames rose higher. "I'll be changing my name," he said.

"To what?"

"Haven't decided yet. My mother's name was Cavendish. I might use that."

"Logan Cavendish," she whispered, liking the sound. "I'll remember."

He bent down and kissed her gently. "Will you, Lizzie?"

"Yes," she promised. "You don't forget the people you love." She regretted the words the minute they left her mouth.

He tilted her chin with his thumb, so she had to look at him. "Love, Lizzie?"

She gazed into his now-familiar face and longed to kiss the frown from his lips. "I didn't mean that the way it sounded."

"There is no *love* between us, Lizzie. It's lust, pure and simple. Because you have no one else and neither do I and we're alone in these damn mountains." He kissed her with a bruising strength, as if to prove his words were true. She leaned against the wall of his chest and took what he gave without pulling away. Heat rose between them, intense and swift, as the kiss deepened into a prelude to lovemaking.

He pushed her onto her back, cradling her against the hard ground. Her hand snaked between the unfastened sections of his coat and found him, hard and ready. He unfastened her clothing, she pulled his shirt from his waistband and fumbled with his clothing until she touched him, hard and warm, with her fingers.

Logan lowered himself carefully above her. "Lust," he murmured, brushing his lips against hers as he found the moist warmth between her thighs. "You're ready for me already."

She urged him closer. "And you are ready for me."

He slid into her with an easy grace. Tight and slick, she was made for him. Love didn't have anything to do with it, he reminded himself as he withdrew slowly, then penetrated again.

The sensation made him dizzy with pleasure, so he closed his eyes against the last rays of daylight and moved within this woman who gave him her body and now her heart.

Long minutes later, when he had brought her satisfaction and reached his own heart-pounding climax, Logan lifted himself from her and readjusted his clothing.

Elizabeth sat up. "Did the biscuits burn?" Her voice was shaky.

Logan turned to her, noting he had reddened her chin with his whiskers again. She was beautiful, calmly buttoning her shirt with trembling fingers and pretending she wasn't still quivering from what they had just experienced. He reached for her and stilled her hands within his.

"Look at me, Lizzie." He waited until she complied before continuing. "I want you to know—" Logan stopped, then began again. "I want you to know. If I was ever going to love someone, it would be you."

"You don't know me." Disbelief colored her voice. "You don't know anything about me."

"I know what I need to know," he said quietly. "And I would love you, if I could."

STARS DOTTED the dark sky when Logan finished taking care of the horses and finally lay beside Elizabeth. She had been waiting for him, knowing she couldn't fall asleep without knowing he was beside her. He held her in his arms and she relaxed in his embrace.

"One more night on the trail," Logan told her. "Then we'll be in Pocatello."

Elizabeth wondered why she wasn't happier with the news. "Aren't you afraid to go into a town?"

"Only a few people know I'm coming," he assured her. "And they can be trusted."

"But what about the marshal who was looking for you? And the bounty hunter?"

"The boys were taking care of that. They were going to pretend to spot me in Salt Lake, heading south to Saint George. The law will expect me to head for the southern border or into the wilds of Wyoming Territory. Besides, we've spent extra days up in these mountains. They most likely will have given up by now."

She didn't believe him. Men would wait a long time for a chance at fifteen thousand dollars. "Why Pocatello? Why don't you just go on to Montana?"

He chuckled. "I'm not riding to Montana on the back of a horse, Lizzie. I'm going to take the train north to Helena, just like everyone else."

"Isn't that going to be dangerous?"

"As long as it's not the Southern Pacific, sweetheart, I'll be fine."

Elizabeth listened as his breathing deepened and steadied. She had the disturbing feeling that it wasn't going to be as easy as Logan thought. And knowing him, he wasn't going to worry her. Not even if they were walking into a hornet's nest of trouble.

He had something to do in Pocatello. Something important, something worth risking his life for. Elizabeth closed her eyes and willed herself to sleep quickly. There was no sense worrying. It wasn't her problem, after all. She'd be on a train and what happened to Logan Younger would be none of her concern.

But she wished she could talk him out of it.

THE NEXT DAY'S TRAVEL brought them farther into Idaho. It was another long day, and they made camp in a secluded grove long before sundown. The next morning, Elizabeth stopped beside Logan on a ridge and, facing west, saw the broad basin in the distance. The ride down the mountain was slow, and there were many times Elizabeth clung to the saddlehorn and prayed the horse wouldn't lose his balance and plunge them both over the steep mountainside.

They passed several ranches on their way through the wide basin. Even the horses seemed pleased to be on flat ground once again and looked around curiously as they headed northwest.

Pocatello turned out to be a railroad town, a place where the two tracks of the Northern Pacific intersected. Logan hesitated at the edge of civilization and eyed the brown buildings in the distance, then checked his revolvers.

"Are you worried?" she asked.

"Just cautious," he muttered, urging his horse to a walk.

Elizabeth reluctantly followed him. "We're just going to ride down the middle of Main Street? Somehow that doesn't seem like the best plan."

"There's only one plan."

She leaned forward, not wanting to miss a word. "Which is?"

"Getting out of here alive."

"Well, I knew *that*."

"Shut up and don't do anything to attract attention. Stay behind me. I don't want you blocking my sight."

Elizabeth would have given her only pair of boots to know what or who was so important in Pocatello. The town, with its dusty street and wooden buildings, looked like something out of a John Wayne movie. It was Saturday, she realized, and as they approached the houses on the outskirts of town, Elizabeth saw people. There were women doing ordinary things, like digging in gardens and calling children to come home. She saw Logan watching them, too, almost as if he was looking for someone. His expression had changed, from grim watchfulness to a kind of submerged excitement.

He led them through the busy streets and no one paid them the least bit of attention. It seemed that a railroad town was accustomed to strangers. Logan paused in front of a hotel.

"Are we going to stay here?" Since they hadn't been shot at or arrested, Elizabeth began to dream of a hot bath and a soft mattress. They'd passed a mercantile, so maybe she could even buy a dress and a decent bonnet. She had her hundred dollars from the poker game and she was determined to dress like everyone else. Surely she could travel from Pocatello to Salt Lake without attracting attention of any kind.

"Unless you'd prefer sleeping in the street." He winked at her and got off his horse, then tied both animals to the hitching post while Elizabeth managed an awkward dismount. Logan threw the saddlebags over his shoulder and headed for the double doors of the hotel, Elizabeth hurrying to keep up. She waited in the lobby, watching for anyone who looked like a bounty hunter or wore a star on his chest, while Logan registered at the front desk. Again, no one paid any attention to them. Laughter came from somewhere in the back of the room and she could hear the tinkle of glassware. She watched as Logan handed the hotel manager the dusty pair of saddlebags and assumed Logan was having his money put in a safe.

"Come on," he said, motioning toward the staircase. "I've arranged for hot water to be sent up in ten minutes."

Elizabeth paused at the landing. "Can I shop first?"

"Shop?"

"I can't take a bath and put these clothes back on. And I can't sit around wrapped in a shawl, either. I'm going to need a dress for the train. I saw a mercantile next door."

Logan's gaze flickered over the crowd in the lobby and then settled on her. "You have money?"

She discreetly patted her bosom. "Tucked away in a safe place."

His voice dropped to a whisper. "We're in room twelve. You're Mrs. Cavendish and we're here to take the train to Portland."

"We're sharing a room?"

His eyes narrowed. "You have a problem with that?"

She smiled up at him. "No. I've discovered I like sleeping with you."

"Good." He took her elbow and guided her to the door. "Fifteen minutes, Lizzie. Then I'm going to assume you're in trouble and come after you."

"I'll be careful," she promised. "I just want to spend some money."

He sighed, then opened the door for her. "I'm coming with you. I've just decided I need a new shirt."

"You don't trust me?"

Logan smiled and stepped out onto the boardwalk. "Lady, I trust you, but I'll be damned if I'll trust anyone else in this town."

"You just want to see what I'm buying."

"Could be. Maybe I want some new duds, too." They stopped in front of the mercantile and Logan opened the door and ushered her inside the cool dark building. "We might as well look as good as we can, I guess."

11

HE LOOKED pretty damn good, Elizabeth decided. They both did, although she wished she could have done something more stylish with her hair than pull it back with a length of yellow grosgrain. She'd spent a luxurious hour bathing in a tin tub brought to the room and filled with steaming water. She'd washed her hair and scrubbed her fingernails. The hotel maid had supplied sweet-smelling soap and clean towels, both heavenly advantages to civilization, and Elizabeth had taken her time donning her new clothes. The wound had healed, and she had no trouble using her arm again.

She'd wanted to look her best for her last night with Logan, though she didn't want to think of never seeing him again. Minute by minute, she promised herself. That was the way she would experience these last hours with the man she'd grown to love.

Logan stood in front of her. He was wearing new dark slacks and a creamy shirt, a string bow tie and a black jacket that gave him the look of a prosperous rancher ready for a night on the town. He had on a new black hat and his hair was trimmed neatly above his collar. But the most amazing difference was the absence of the familiar beard.

Clean-shaven and somehow younger-looking, he now resembled the man who had spirited her out of the Salt Lake hotel, not the grungy outlaw who'd led her over a mountain range, nursed her through a bullet wound and made love to her by the campfire.

"You're a very good-looking man, especially when you're cleaned up," Elizabeth told him.

Logan looked surprised. "I'm not much for new clothes," he said. "Haven't had too many."

"Well, you look good in them." She picked up her skirt and twirled around. "What do you think? Do I look like a fashionable eighties lady?"

His hands spanned the slim waistline that dropped to her hips in a flattering line. "Yellow and blue. Spring colors. They suit you."

"Thank you, sir." She smiled up at him and he bent down to kiss her upturned lips. "I think we make a very handsome couple."

"And so do I, Miss Lizzie. You're quite beautiful in that dress."

"Do you think anyone will recognize us?"

"No." He shook his head. "There's no one here to care. After I stabled the horses, I had a drink at the saloon next door and listened to the talk. The sheriff had to go off somewhere. A marshal was through here days ago asking questions, but he went back to Utah empty-handed. We might as well be a thousand miles from Utah, instead of across the border."

"We're really safe?"

He nodded. "I'd like to think so. Besides, no one is going to recognize you as the woman at the robbery."

"I'm more worried about *you*."

"The law will expect me to head for the southern border or into the wilds of Wyoming Territory."

Elizabeth wanted to believe him, but she wondered if it was that easy. They'd spent day after day looking over their shoulders. It was difficult to relax now. "But what about the bounty hunter?"

"There's been no sign of that bastard, but I can't pretend I wouldn't like a shot at him."

"You're supposed to be through with all that."

He smiled at her. "I'm glad you keep reminding me."

The tension she'd felt since entering the town eased a little. "I have to find out about the train to Salt Lake."

Logan's smile faded. "I did that already. Tomorrow. There's a train at noon. You can be on it, if that's what you want."

"All right." One more day. One more day she hadn't expected, and the knowledge made her feel unexpectedly lighthearted, as if she'd been given a reprieve. "Can we go out for dinner?"

Logan shook his head. "Not yet. There's something I have to do first."

"What?"

"Someone I have to see."

This was it, then. The reason for the excitement, the reason he'd shaved and bought new clothes. A man went to that much trouble for a job interview or a woman. She knew Logan wasn't looking for employment opportunities. Elizabeth gulped. She'd be damned if she would ask for more information. "All right. I'll walk around town a little bit. It will be interesting to see in person what I've only seen in the movies."

His eyebrows rose. "You can't walk around this town alone, especially on a Saturday night."

"Why not?"

"It's not done," he sputtered. "You'll look like a—" He stopped, his face flushed, and took her hand. "Stay here, Lizzie. I'll order some supper for you and I'll be back as soon as I can."

Her heart fell and she told herself it was ridiculous to feel so disappointed. She had nothing to do with the rest of Logan's life. From the moment she stepped onto the train, whatever he did would not concern her. She would take her book and return to the future that waited for her. Her gaze shifted to her saddlebag, leaning against the side of the bed. It held *Rogues Across Time,* her paisley shawl and the worn bonnet. Souvenirs of a trip no one would ever believe, she realized, and therefore meaningless to anyone else.

"Okay. I'll wait for you to come back," she said. "Maybe I'll read."

His eyes narrowed. "That book?"

She went over to the bag and pulled out the battered book. The vibration between her fingers was stronger than she'd felt since appearing in this century. Startled, Elizabeth dropped it and it crashed at her feet.

"What the hell—" Logan was beside her in two strides. "You've gone all white, like you're going to swoon."

She closed her eyes and waited for the dizziness to pass while Logan took her into his arms and held her.

"Elizabeth?" he said. "Talk to me. Are you sick?"

"No." She looked up at him. "The book—"

Logan eased her to the bed and made her sit down. Then he picked up the book from the floor and snapped it shut. "What's the matter with it?"

"You don't feel anything?"

"No." He tossed it on the bed.

"Pick it up," she demanded, moving away from it. "Take it off the bed."

He shot her a curious look and carefully replaced the book in the leather bag. "You going to tell me what's going on?"

"It vibrated, just the way it did...before."

Logan frowned. "Before you came here?"

"Yes. I thought it was my imagination, that I was overtired, but it happened again." She lifted her gaze to his worried eyes. "I'm in a hotel again, Logan. Maybe it will work. Maybe I won't have to go back to the same place in Salt Lake."

"You're not going anywhere. Not tonight, anyway." He pulled the shawl from the bag and tossed it to her, then took her wrist and pulled her to her feet. "You're coming with me."

"I am?"

"I can't leave you here," he growled. "Not with that damn book, anyway. We're going to get out of here."

Elizabeth hesitated as she wrapped the light fabric around her shoulders. "Are you sure I won't be in the way?" As much as she wanted to go with him, she didn't especially relish being a witness to some romantic reunion.

"No. Maybe you'll help." He ushered her out the door and locked it behind him.

"Who is she?"

"Not a she. He. Danny," he explained, pocketing the key in his new black vest. "My son."

LOGAN WANTED a drink, but he passed by the saloon with little more than a wistful glance and kept Elizabeth from gawking inside by keeping a grip on her arm. No one seemed to notice them, except for a cowboy who tipped his hat to Elizabeth and walked past. They looked like any couple out for a stroll before sundown. He liked that. He liked her new bonnet, too. Trimmed to match her dress, the stripes gave her a jaunty look.

She'd been silent since they walked down the stairs and through the crowded lobby. Elizabeth was smart enough to keep her mouth shut in crowds, something he appreciated in a woman. He kept his hand on her elbow and watched for the side street that would take him to his son.

"Tell me about him," she said. They were out of sight now, heading down a narrow dirt street. "How old is he?"

"He'll be ten next month."

"And where has he been all this time?"

"When I was in prison, you mean?" She nodded, and he continued. "Sarah's sister took him. Her husband works for the Northern Pacific now, so they moved here a few years ago."

"When was the last time you saw him?"

"The day I buried his mother."

Elizabeth squeezed his arm in silent sympathy. "Does he know you're coming?"

"I sent a wire." Logan's footsteps quickened. The man at the front desk said it was a two-story white house next to a large shed and a place that fit that description was up ahead, on the left side of the street. He knew he was making it difficult for Elizabeth to keep up with his steps, but he couldn't help hurrying. A few more yards and he'd be able to see Danny again. Did he still look like Sarah?

As they approached the house, Logan thought his heart would pound clear out of his chest. He hadn't been this nervous since the time he'd robbed his first train, east of Sacramento. The boy wouldn't recognize him, not after all these years.

"I'll wait here," Elizabeth offered, stopping at the foot of the steps to the front porch. "You go ahead."

He took the steps two at a time and knocked on the door with more force than he'd intended. The door swung open and a small round woman stood staring up at him. She wore a white apron over a green calico dress and there was a smudge of flour on her cheek. Logan quickly removed his hat. "Martha?"

The wary expression in her blue eyes softened, but she didn't smile. "Logan. We'd wondered what happened to you."

She could have been referring to the last ten days, since he'd sent the telegram, but he didn't think so. "A lot has happened these past years," he admitted. "There were things I had to take care of."

"I heard you'd gone bad."

Logan twisted the brim of his hat between his fingers. "No, Martha. I had some getting even to do. You know what the railroad took from me."

"And now you're an outlaw. A wanted man."

"Not anymore, Martha. I served my time and I got even with the railroad. I'm going to buy a ranch in eastern Montana and settle—"

She raised her hand. "I don't want to know. It's better that I don't."

"All right." He peered over her shoulder into the parlor, but the room was empty. "Can I see him?"

"He's out back feeding the chickens." She stepped aside to allow him to enter, but Logan hesitated.

"I brought someone—"

Martha looked past him and her expression brightened. "Logan! You should have told me that you were married."

"I'm not," he replied. "She's a good friend of mine. I'll bring her inside, too, if you don't mind."

"What kind of friend?"

He held her shocked gaze. "A special friend, Martha. I'm planning to ask her to head north with me, but I don't think she'll say yes."

Martha continued to frown as Logan gestured to Elizabeth to join him.

"Elizabeth, I'd like you to meet my sister-in-law, Martha Sherman. Martha, this is Elizabeth."

Martha reluctantly took Elizabeth's outstretched hand. "How nice to meet you, Miss—"

"Cavendish," Elizabeth filled in for her.

"I'm using that name now," Logan explained as they entered the front room. "It's safer."

"I see." Martha looked from one to the other. Clearly, she didn't approve of the situation, but Logan wasn't about to apologize for anything. Living in sin sure as hell wasn't the worst thing he'd ever done in his life, and he figured even the Lord might forgive him for kidnapping a woman from another century and falling in love with her, too. Letting her go would be punishment enough for his sins.

Logan took a deep breath. "Does Danny remember me?"

"Of course." She gestured toward the narrow sofa. "Please, uh, Mrs. Cavendish, sit down."

"Thank you."

"I'll call him." Martha hurried out of the room, to the back of the house.

Logan ignored Elizabeth's questioning glance and concentrated on watching the doorway to the dining room. He stood in the middle of the cozy room and waited. There were sounds of footsteps upstairs and the high-pitched screeches of small children. Martha's oldest, a solemn little girl, was a year older than Danny. There were others now, he realized, from the shrieking upstairs. Danny had grown up with other children. Would he want to leave this house and set off alone with only his father for company?

"It will be all right," Elizabeth assured him. He didn't answer, because he watched as a gangly boy with sandy hair came toward him. Dark blue eyes, angular face, skinnier than Logan had pictured. The boy didn't smile, but he didn't take his gaze from Logan's face, either.

Logan swallowed his terror and held out his hand. "Danny?"

"Yes, sir."

"Do you know who I am?"

The boy stopped three feet away. "Yes, sir."

Logan dropped his hand and wished like hell he knew what to do. The kid stared at him as if Logan had three heads. "Did your Aunt Martha tell you I was coming?"

"Yes, sir."

"You look like your mother."

"Yes, sir."

Well, so far, the only thing he knew was that Danny knew two words. Logan took another step toward the boy—*his son*—and paused. He wanted to wrap him in his arms and hold on to him. He wanted to lift him in the air and swing him around until the boy screamed with delight, the way he'd done the morning before the railroad men arrived with their guns and their land deeds. But this boy didn't look as if he would let his father touch him. The expression in his eyes remained guarded.

Logan reached into his pocket and pulled out a packet of licorice. "I remembered you liked these."

"Thanks." The boy took the candy, but didn't say anything more.

Elizabeth broke the silence. "Hi, Danny," she said, smiling. "I'm Elizabeth, a . . . friend of your father's." She patted the empty place beside her on the couch. "Come here and tell me about Pocatello. I've never been here before."

The boy carefully circumvented his father and obeyed Elizabeth's command. He sat gingerly on the sofa and looked at the woman next to him. "It's not much of a town."

Logan turned to watch both of them. At least the boy knew more words.

"Is there a school?"

"Yes, ma'am. I can read and write pretty good."

Elizabeth murmured something about school while Logan watched. Had Danny read of his father's activities? Logan wondered if his son had seen the wanted notice with his picture on it. He'd never pictured Danny as old enough to realize what had been happening these past years. He was a damn fool to think his own son wouldn't know who he was and what he'd become.

They both looked up at him, as if waiting for him to say something, but Logan had been lost in thought while they were talking. Elizabeth took pity on him and repeated the question.

"Why don't you tell Danny about Montana?" She nodded her encouragement after Logan paused.

"I'm going to build a ranch," he replied, watching the boy's eyes light up with delight.

"With horses?" Danny asked.

"Yeah." Logan hid a smile. "A ranch has to have horses."

Logan hesitated, afraid to say anything more. Elizabeth and Danny turned those blue eyes on him and froze him to the rug. Elizabeth's eyebrows rose and she frowned at him, then opened her mouth to say something. Martha, wiping her hands on her apron, hurried into the room with two little girls beside her.

"Abigail and Charity, say hello to your uncle and Mrs. Cavendish." She pushed them forward and the children giggled. Danny smiled and the smaller child hurried over to him and climbed on his lap as Logan watched. Clearly, his son had been raised well by Sarah's sister.

"You'll stay for dinner," she said. "Please don't say no. We've been looking forward to your arrival for over a week now, and Bert will be disappointed if you leave before he comes home."

"Thank you," Elizabeth answered for both of them. "We'd be pleased to stay."

Logan raised his gaze to the small woman. "I owe you a great deal, Martha."

"I've raised him as my own," she replied. "It was what Sarah would have wanted."

"Yes," he agreed, turning to his son. The boy was whispering something into the little girl's ear and she was giggling with delight. "It was what Sarah would have wanted."

HE'D GONE quiet again. Elizabeth walked beside Logan in silence along the dark street. When they turned onto the more raucous and active Main Street, Logan ignored the other men lounging outside the saloon and guided Elizabeth to the hotel in the safety of darkness.

Once in their room, with the lamp lit, she was able to see the lines of strain that etched his mouth. His expression was bleak, a startling contrast to the excitement she'd seen on his face earlier.

Elizabeth removed her bonnet and tossed her shawl over a chair. "He's a fine boy."

"Yes." Logan stood at the window and pulled the lace curtain aside to look down into the street. "A fine boy," he repeated, his voice grim.

She sat on the edge of the bed and watched him. "You didn't tell him about Montana."

The outlaw shrugged. "Guess not."

"You came here to get him, didn't you?"

"Yeah." He laughed, a harsh sound in the quiet room. "It took me months to find out where he was. With Bert working for the railroad, they moved around a lot. That's why I was in Salt Lake. I'd learned where Danny was and I wired Martha that I was coming."

"They seemed like nice people."

He turned away from the window and sank into the oak chair in the corner. "He doesn't belong with me anymore."

"He's your son."

"But he's part of their family. He has sisters. A real home. He goes to school. I can't take him away from all of this."

"But what if he wants to go?"

Logan shook his head. "He barely spoke to me."

"He doesn't know you," Elizabeth countered. "He's shy. I watched him. Danny looked at you when you weren't watching, as if he couldn't believe you were real."

He leaned back and closed his eyes, as weary as if he had just walked a hundred miles. "All this time, I thought, we'd be together, the two of us. Father and son, building something together. Something that would make up for all the years we lost."

Elizabeth went over to him, knelt at his feet and took his hand. "And you will," she promised.

"No. I can't take him away from what he has now."

"Look at me." She waited until she had his attention before she continued. "I was raised in foster homes. I never knew who my father was, and my mother made a lot of promises she couldn't keep because she drank too much. We lived in shelters, when we were lucky." It was easier than she thought to say the words she'd never before said to anyone. His gray-eyed gaze didn't embarrass her; she didn't feel humiliated or degraded. The truth was the truth, she realized. And it didn't hurt to tell it. "She drank so much she forgot she had a child," Elizabeth told him. "And the state took me away from her and I never saw her again. I spent my life hoping someone would care about me. I've been on my own since the day I was eighteen. And I've never told anyone what I just told you."

"You're a fine woman," Logan said. "You've nothing to be ashamed about."

"I never wanted anyone to know," she admitted. "I made up a family. I even bought antiques that I pretended had been in my family for generations. That's why I bought that book."

"And the man you're going to marry?"

"He doesn't know."

Logan frowned. "It won't matter to him. Not if he's any kind of man at all."

"I don't want him to be ashamed of me. He comes from a good family in Boston. He's a man who has had every advantage since the day he was born. I don't think he'd understand."

"There's no cause for shame, Lizzie," Logan repeated. "You had no say in your life when you were a child."

Elizabeth smiled up at him. "Exactly. And neither has Danny. Up until now, that is."

"What are you getting at?"

"Give the boy a choice, Logan. Let him decide if he wants to stay with Martha or go with you. Maybe he wants to be with his father. You're a good man, and he must have memories of happy times with you."

"He knows I'm an outlaw."

"Maybe. But you can explain to him that that part of your life is over, can't you?"

There was a long silence. Logan played with her hair, untied the ribbon and combed his fingers through the dark waves. "When Bert and I went out onto the porch after dinner, he told me they'd tried to keep the truth from Danny, but he wasn't sure what the boy knew."

"I like Bert. He seems like a nice man."

"He's been a good father to my son," Logan said. "He offered to keep him, if that's what I wanted. Though he said he understood a man wanting his son. I got the feeling Martha doesn't think I'm good enough to have him. I'll tell you, Lizzie, that's what hurts more than anything."

"They love him. And so do you. He's a lucky boy."

"I keep thinking of what Sarah would want."

"She would want her two men to be together, I think."

Logan sighed. "I just want to do what's right. For a change," he added.

"You will," she assured him. "And if you take Danny with you, you'll take good care of him. Just like you've taken good care of me." She smiled up at him again.

"You'll teach him to be a good man, just like his father."

He bent his head to kiss her. "Thank you."

"For what?"

"I've been alone for so long, I forgot there's any other way of thinking but my own." He wrapped his arms around her and pulled her onto his lap. Elizabeth leaned her head on his strong shoulder and began to relax. For the first time in her life, she felt at ease. It didn't matter anymore if she didn't know who her father was or that her mother had abandoned her when she was six. It didn't matter that she didn't have a family, that she had never belonged anywhere. For now, just this little while, she belonged with Logan.

And that was enough.

ELIZABETH LAY IN BED the next morning and listened to Logan's even breathing. She was facing the window, and Logan's warm body was cupped around hers, his large hands holding her close against him while he slept. She should have felt peaceful, but peace was the last thing on her mind. This was the last day. Today, the noon train would lead her from Logan, and rightfully so. He had another life to live, one that would take him to a ranch in Montana. She hoped he'd take Danny with him.

And she had another life to live also. If there had been any doubt in her mind before, the incident with the book yesterday had dispelled it. There had been something magic, something powerful that vibrated through her fingers when she'd touched it. Perhaps she could have taken the book to bed with her last night and awakened in her own time this morning, but she'd taken Logan to bed with her instead.

They hadn't made love last night. They'd held each other tightly and slept. She'd been grateful he hadn't saddled his horse and ridden out of her life. Because, despite his insistence that he was safe, that no one was following him, Elizabeth couldn't quite bring herself to believe that was true. She'd felt someone's gaze on her neck when they'd entered the hotel yesterday, and she'd caught a man turning away from them quickly, as if he couldn't afford to be seen.

"What's wrong?" Logan murmured, tightening his arm around her. "You're trembling."

"What if there's someone following us?"

He yawned. "Why would you think that? We traveled for days with no one but Billy to bother us."

"I don't know. Since we got to town, I've had the feeling we're being watched. Don't you feel it?"

"No." He kissed her neck. "Mmm. You taste good."

"Someone could know that there's a price on your head. Even if you don't look like an outlaw anymore."

"I can take care of myself, Lizzie. Anyone who wants a fight will get one." He nibbled her earlobe. "And they won't win." His warm hands roamed down her new cotton nightgown and caressed her breasts. "We're safe," he whispered. "In a warm bed with all the time in the world."

Elizabeth swallowed her worry and turned onto her back. "Is that a hint?"

"Yes, ma'am," he drawled, covering her mouth with his.

12

"STAY WITH ME," he said long after their bodies separated and their breathing had returned to normal.

"What?"

He rolled over on his side and faced her. "Stay with me, Lizzie. Don't go back."

She closed her eyes and fought the familiar stabbing pain that accompanied every thought of leaving him. "I can't."

"Look at me," Logan ordered. She did, wishing to memorize his face. "We're good together."

"By accident," Elizabeth countered. "A twist of fate."

"So?" He frowned. "What difference does that make? We're together, and it's good. Come to Montana with me."

"I can't," she repeated. "I have a life—"

"A life you lie about," he finished for her.

She rolled away from him and left the bed. "I shouldn't have told you all that."

"Why not? Why are you ashamed of who you are?"

She wrapped her shawl around her naked body as if to defend herself from his questions. "I'm not ashamed," she managed to say, although unshed tears thickened her throat.

He sat up and glared across the room at her. "Last night, you told me you lie about who you are and where you come from. You should be proud of what you've survived and what you've made of yourself. The fool you're marrying should feel the same way."

"Next week," Elizabeth whispered. "I'm getting married next week. The past won't matter anymore."

"And what about *now?*" Logan climbed off the bed and, splendidly naked, stood in front of her. He flung his arm to encompass the room. "And what about this?" he asked. "Is all of this going to be forgotten, too?"

She shook her head. "I love you," she whispered, her eyes swimming in tears. "I couldn't forget that."

"You're going to leave me and marry someone else."

"I can't stay here."

"Why not?"

"I don't belong here. This isn't my life, Logan. This is yours."

"Ours," he insisted. "It's *our* life."

She reached out and touched his face. The skin was brown from hundreds of days in the Utah sun. She brushed her palm against the stubble of beard and felt the tickle against her skin. "No," she said. "My life isn't here. I've worked too hard to lose everything now."

He turned from her and grabbed his pants from the chair. He dressed quickly, in silence, and so did she. Elizabeth blinked back the tears and found her new hairbrush. They would dress, then go downstairs to the dining room for breakfast. Later on this morning, he would take her to the train station. At noon, she would leave. And if everything worked out the way she thought it would, she would wake up tomorrow in Boston. In 1996.

"What if it doesn't work, Lizzie?" Logan turned and watched her tie the ribbon at the nape of her neck. He was thinking along the same lines that she was, she realized.

"The book has to work."

"No," he said. "It doesn't. You could wake up in Salt Lake tomorrow morning and it would be 1886."

Elizabeth couldn't answer. She wouldn't let herself consider that possibility, though, of course, it existed.

"I can't take the risk of staying here," he told her. "I'm leaving when you are, and I don't know where I'll end up."

"I could find out from Martha."

"You heard her. She doesn't want to know."

"She'll know, if you do what you should do and take your son with you."

Logan turned away without answering. "I'll meet you downstairs for breakfast," he said, and left the room.

HOTCAKES AND EGGS didn't settle the tension in her stomach. Elizabeth pushed away her plate, still piled high with food, and asked the waitress for a cup of tea. Logan ate his breakfast with steady determination and no sign of enjoyment. She waited for him to finish and looked around the crowded dining room. A few women, obviously hotel guests, dined with men who looked like husbands. Elizabeth assumed they were railroad passengers, passing through on their way to somewhere else. Logan had explained that the town was a place where two railroad lines crossed.

The rest of the tables were filled with an odd assortment of men. Elizabeth felt as if someone was staring at her, and supposed she should expect it. The 1880s wasn't exactly an enlightened age. She wondered if women had won the right to vote yet.

The feeling of foreboding wouldn't go away. Elizabeth spent the rest of the morning packing her few possessions into the new valise they'd purchased. She'd handled *Rogues Across Time* gingerly; the vibrations had almost numbed her fingers and she'd dropped it carefully in the small valise. Then she paced back and forth across the bedroom, waiting for something terrible to happen.

Logan retrieved his money, still tucked in the worn saddlebags, from the hotel safe and packed up his things. "I paid the hotel bill," he said, then looked at his watch. "We should get out of here in about fifteen minutes. The station isn't far away, but I'll feel better when we're looking at a train." He frowned, watching her walk around the room. "Is your arm hurting?"

"No." At least that was the truth. She went to the window again and stared down at the empty street below. She didn't know what she expected to see. It wasn't as if a federal marshal would advertise his presence to the man he was going to arrest. He certainly wouldn't stand outside on the street and flash his badge in warning.

Logan came up behind her and put his arms around her waist. Elizabeth leaned back into the comforting wall of his chest. "There's nothing out there," he said.

"I'd like to believe that."

"Then do." He rested his chin on the top of her head.

"Why aren't you worried?"

He sighed. "I'm out of Utah, I'm away from the Southern Pacific Railroad. I feel like I can breathe for the first time in my life." He kissed the top of her head. "Even the sheriff is out of town. How lucky can I get?"

"Take him with you, Logan." She turned in his arms and looked up into his shadowed gray eyes. His mouth tightened. He knew she wasn't talking about the sheriff.

He dropped his arms and took a step back. "I told you, it's none of your concern what I do with my son."

She ignored the cutting words. "You belong together. Promise me you'll take him with you."

"I don't make promises I can't keep."

"He loves you."

His mouth thinned. "He shouldn't."

"Why not?"

"I'll send for him," Logan promised, ignoring the question. "When I have a home for him."

"When?"

He shrugged. "As long as it takes."

"But what if it takes years? He'll be a teenager then, and he'll have spent too many years thinking his father didn't want him. It will be too late."

"Yeah, well, it's too late for a lot of things."

"You don't believe that."

Logan moved away and fastened his shoulder holster, then checked his revolvers.

"I thought you weren't expecting trouble."

"Habit," he murmured. He put on his coat and immediately looked like a prosperous rancher. Then Logan picked up their belongings and opened the door. "It's time to go," he said. He turned, confident that she would follow him. Elizabeth took one last look around the room before she walked through the open doorway. It was over; she could delay no longer. Logan Younger would go on with his life, in whatever way he chose. And she would do everything in her power to return to the life she'd created one hundred years in the future.

She would deal with her broken heart later.

THE LARGE WOODEN STATION was crowded with people of all kinds. Logan looked around and saw cowboys, men dressed in suits and women in dresses and hats. Women were wearing that odd dress with the bustle attached. Elizabeth looked like any other woman at the station, except she was the most beautiful. Men looked at her, then saw Logan's warning glare and quickly looked away. Satisfied, Logan touched Elizabeth's waist and guided her toward the ticket counter.

"Folks like to come watch the trains," the ticket master explained as Logan commented on the crowd. "How can I help you folks?"

"I'd like one ticket north to Helena," Logan drawled. He looked at Elizabeth, but she didn't say anything. He turned back to the uniformed man. "And one to Ogden, with a connection to Salt Lake, for the lady."

"You'll have to change trains," the man informed her.

"That's fine," Elizabeth agreed, but her voice was shaky. She stood quietly beside Logan as he paid for the tickets and handed her the ones that would take her away from him.

"The train to Helena departs at twelve thirty-two."

"And the one to Ogden?" Logan hoped it was delayed.

The man glanced up at the oversize clock on the wall above his head. "That one should be arriving in about fifteen minutes. Departure is set for noon."

Logan swallowed the lump in his throat and took Elizabeth's arm. Fifteen minutes to convince her to change her mind. He wished he could tell her what she meant to him. He wished he could take his son and his woman and head north, to live a peaceful life.

A peaceful life. Was there any such thing? Logan quickly scanned the crowd for any sign of danger. Elizabeth's worries had spooked him. It was that damn book's fault. If he believed it had brought her to him, he had to believe it would take her away, into another world, another century.

He wished he'd burned it when he'd had the chance.

They made their way through the crowd to the wide wooden platform that fronted the empty tracks. Logan paused, bitter disappointment flooding through him at the thought of leaving Pocatello alone. He'd always thought his son would be by his side. And now he'd grown used to protecting Elizabeth and he wasn't real sure she could take care of herself.

"Here," he said, reaching under his jacket. He pulled out one of his revolvers and handed it to her. "Take this. You might need it."

Elizabeth looked as if he were handing her a coiled snake. "I can't take that on the plane," she said.

He ignored her gibberish and thrust the gun into her purse. "If anyone lays a hand on you, shoot him." At her shocked look, he added, "You don't have to kill him. Just wound him a little, just so he gets the message."

Elizabeth nodded, still looking a bit uncertain.

"Chances are, you'll have no trouble, but it won't hurt to carry a little protection."

"Thank you," she said.

"Remember what I taught you."

"I will." She looked past him and her eyes widened. "Logan—"

She pointed toward the corner of the building and Logan turned to see a dark-haired young boy gazing at the crowd as if he was searching for someone.

"He's looking for you, Logan," she said, but that was already obvious as Danny's expression brightened when he caught sight of his father.

"Wait here," Logan said, but Elizabeth followed him, anyway, as he threaded through the crowd toward his son.

Danny eyed him a bit uncertainly. "You're leavin'," he said flatly. "I thought you came to town to get me."

Logan wanted to take him in his arms and never let him go. "I changed my mind."

Elizabeth gasped. "Logan!" she cried.

The boy flinched, but he didn't take his gaze from his father. "You gonna tell me why?"

Logan put his hands on the boy's thin shoulders. "You've got a good home here. I wouldn't blame you if you wanted to stay."

"I want to go with you," the child insisted. He lifted his bag as proof. "I've packed up. I heard Uncle Bert tell Aunt Martha that you were leaving today on the twelve thirty-two. He said it was a damn shame and Aunt Martha cried and said that Sarah wouldn't like the way everything turned out and she said she was goin' to church to pray. They thought I was still asleep."

"Does she know where you are, son?" *Son.* The word warmed his insides.

"Uh-huh. I left a note while she was visitin' Mrs. Grant."

Logan turned to Elizabeth. "What the hell do I do now?"

She smiled up at him. "I think you two have some talking to do. Maybe there's a later train to Helena today."

Logan turned back to his son. "I'm buying a ranch. That means we have a lot of hard work ahead of us."

The boy's eyes shone. "You want me to go with you and help?"

"Yes. I guess you'd better," he drawled, wanting to throw his brand-new hat in the air with relief and joy. "I'm not getting any younger and a strong young fella like you will sure come in handy."

"Logan—" Elizabeth tugged on his arm. "I have to go—"

He realized the train, its enormous engine steaming and clanging, was pulling into the station. "Wait right here and don't move," he told his son. "I'll be right back."

"You don't have to," Elizabeth protested, but he took her arm and helped her through the crowd to the platform where the conductor lowered the stairs to the train.

"Don't do this, Lizzie," he pleaded, waiting as passengers stepped down to solid ground. In a few minutes, she would be gone and he didn't know if he could bear the thought of life without her. "Don't leave me. Don't marry him. Throw the damn book away and marry me instead."

"I love you," she said, her beautiful blue eyes shimmering with tears. "But I can't live this kind of life, never knowing if a marshal is going to arrest you or someone will pull a gun on you and try to claim reward money. I'm not even sure if I'd make a very good mother." She opened her purse and grabbed a lace-trimmed handkerchief from beneath the gun. "I can't walk around with a revolver in my purse, either," she said. She lifted it out. "Here. Take this thing back."

He ignored it. "I love you, Lizzie. I'm sorry I can't offer you any more than that."

She stared to kiss him one final time as the conductor called, "All aboard!"

Then a shot rang out and Logan crumpled to the ground at her feet.

She cried out, her screams mingling with others around her, and she dropped to her knees and leaned over Logan's inert body. Blood poured from somewhere near his thigh and he was unconscious. She wondered wildly if was dead or if he'd hit his head when he'd fallen and her insides clenched with fear for his life. "Logan!"

She heard a rough voice order, "Get back, damn it," and Elizabeth looked up to see a roughly dressed man in black standing over her. He held a revolver in his right hand and his smile was laced with menace as he looked down at the outlaw. "Well, well," he drawled. "I've been waitin' a long time for this."

"Please," Elizabeth said, sobbing. "Help me."

"Fifteen thousand, dead or alive, the railroad says." The bearded man turned his nasty smile on Elizabeth. His dark eyes glittered with satisfaction. "'Dead' suits me just fine."

"He's not dead," she protested, feeling his heartbeat under her hand. Logan's gun, the one she'd tried to hand him, slid uselessly to the ground by her knees. He wasn't dead, thank God. There was still hope, if she could get him to a doctor. "Someone, help me, please!"

"A shame," the man with the gun murmured. The people in the crowd didn't move.

"My God," she cried as the man smiled again. "Who are you?"

He tilted his hat politely. "Al Richardson, ma'am. At your service."

"The bounty hunter," she said. "You followed us."

"I see my reputation precedes me. And, no, it was not at all necessary to follow anyone anywhere." He smiled, and Elizabeth's blood froze at the evil expression in his black eyes. "I merely read Younger's telegram from Salt Lake and chose to wait for him here. I would have preferred to kill him in a more private place, but I overslept." He lifted his gun and pointed it at Logan's head. "Now, ma'am, if you'll move out of the way, I'll finish this nasty business."

A man stepped forward. "Now, mister, we don't hold with murder in this town."

The bounty hunter pointed his gun at him and gestured for him to move aside. "Get out of the way. I'm an agent for the Southern Pacific and this man is a train robber."

"No," Elizabeth cried. "The railroad stole his farm and killed his wife, too."

"Is that what he told you?" Richardson chuckled. "*I* killed his wife. She came over the hill with a rifle," he explained. "Self-defense." He smiled. "I had no choice." He nodded toward the saddlebag. "Now, lady, hand me those saddlebags and move out of the way. I've gone to a lot of trouble to get the sheriff out of town and that snoopy marshal headed on a wild-goose chase to Ogden. I'm through wasting time."

"Pa!" a child screamed, forcing his way through the crowd that surrounded them. Danny jostled the bounty hunter for a second, giving Elizabeth time to reach for the gun. She pulled back the hammer the way Logan had taught her and put her finger on the trigger.

He smiled, ignored her shaking gun and pointed his revolver toward Logan's skull. "I can kill both of you before you have time to pull the trigger."

"No," she cried as Danny flung his arms around Richardson's knees. She couldn't let him kill the one person she had ever loved, the one person who loved her. Elizabeth tightened her arm and squeezed the trigger and the bounty hunter faltered. His gun fired, the bullet splintering the boards near Logan's head, before the man dropped to the ground.

She thought the sound would split her skull in two, and then she heard nothing. She could see people with their mouths open, she felt Danny's arms around her, she saw Logan's eyelids flicker and close once again and she tried to cry out for help. Bert and Martha frantically shoved their way through the crowd and bent over Logan's body.

"Help me," Elizabeth begged, sobbing. "Please, help me."

Her hearing cleared as Martha pulled her to her feet. "Mrs. Cavendish," the woman said. "Are you all right?"

"I killed a man," she whispered, turning away from the still body of the bounty hunter. Blood poured from his chest, and his eyes were still open, the surprise frozen on his ugly face.

"Yes," Martha said, taking her elbow. "Get on the train, dear. Isn't that what you were supposed to be doing?"

"Yes. I'm going to Salt Lake, then I'm going... home." There was little comfort in the word.

"Perhaps you should do that. Before there are any... complications from this unfortunate incident."

Someone said, "It was self-defense, Mrs. Sherman. The dead man was going to kill us all."

Martha turned her gaze back to Elizabeth. "Be that as it may, perhaps you should leave now, before the law is involved."

"I can't." She watched as Bert and three other men carried Logan carefully through the crowd. Danny was right behind them, carrying his father's bags, carrying their future. "I can't leave him like this. I can't leave him."

"It looks like a thigh wound. The doctor will take care of him. You mustn't worry."

"I can't go," Elizabeth repeated, turning away from the curious gaze of the conductor. "My bag—"

"Is right here," Martha said, handing it to her. Elizabeth pawed through it and found her book wrapped safely in the paisley shawl. She tossed the shawl aside and grabbed the book. She expected the vibrations, but the book was heavy and dull in her hand. Cool to the touch, it filled her with an overwhelming feeling of peace.

There would be no return to Boston, no wedding to John. She realized she'd made her choice when she'd pulled the trigger of the Colt. She'd realized what her life would be like without Logan, and the thought had made her kill to protect him. She wasn't proud of the killing. She hadn't aimed for his heart, but she hoped if there was a God, he would understand that she couldn't let Logan die.

There was a reason she'd been sent here. She'd come a long way—a hundred years—but in doing so, she'd found a love like the kind she had never known before. Only a fool would throw it away.

"I'm no fool," she said out loud, and the heavy sorrow squeezing her heart lifted and disappeared. She smiled at Martha and took the woman's arm to hurry her after the men.

The train pulled out of the station and Elizabeth felt no regret at its departure. No one but Elizabeth noticed when the book dropped to the ground.

Epilogue

Excerpts from the *Pocatello Gazette*, June 23, 1886:

Miss Elizabeth Richardson, formerly of Boston, Massachusetts, and Mr. L. W. Cavendish, of Montana, were married yesterday in a ceremony at the home of Mr. and Mrs. Bertrand Sherman. The couple, along with Mr. Cavendish's son, will leave on their wedding trip to Helena, Montana, as soon as the groom recovers from gunshot wounds inflicted on June 2, 1886.

Judge Manning ruled that the shooting of Albert Richardson, also known as Bad Al, was justifiable and in self-defense. Miss E. Richardson—no relation to Bad Al—was cleared of all charges. A reward of two thousand dollars for Bad Al's capture—or killing—was recovered from Kansas authorities and presented to Miss Richardson, who professed her shock and gratitude.

Mayor Johnson's wife has announced that an anonymous donation of two thousand dollars has been made to the Women's Suffrage Movement in Idaho and Utah territories.

Found: one book, approximately 7" × 9" and brown with gold inlaid lettering, at the Pocatello Railroad Station. See ticket agent for more information.

BRIDE'S BAY RESORT

UNLOCK THE DOOR TO GREAT ROMANCE AT BRIDE'S BAY RESORT

Join Harlequin's new across-the-lines series, set in an exclusive hotel on an island off the coast of South Carolina.

Seven of your favorite authors will bring you exciting stories about fascinating heroes and heroines discovering love at Bride's Bay Resort.

Look for these fabulous stories coming to a store near you beginning in January 1996.

Harlequin American Romance #613 in January
Matchmaking Baby by Cathy Gillen Thacker

Harlequin Presents #1794 in February
Indiscretions by Robyn Donald

Harlequin Intrigue #362 in March
Love and Lies by Dawn Stewardson

Harlequin Romance #3404 in April
Make Believe Engagement by Day Leclaire

Harlequin Temptation #588 in May
Stranger in the Night by Roseanne Williams

Harlequin Superromance #695 in June
Married to a Stranger by Connie Bennett

Harlequin Historicals #324 in July
Dulcie's Gift by Ruth Langan

Visit Bride's Bay Resort each month wherever
Harlequin books are sold.

HARLEQUIN ®

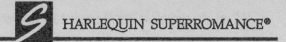

HARLEQUIN SUPERROMANCE®

From the bestselling author of
THE TAGGARTS OF TEXAS!
comes

Cupid, Colorado...

This is ranch country, cowboy country—a land of high mountains
and swift, cold rivers, of deer, elk and bear. The land is important
here—family and neighbors are, too. 'Course, you have the chance
to really get to know your neighbors in Cupid. Take the Camerons,
for instance. The first Cameron came to Cupid more than a hundred
years ago, and Camerons have owned and worked the Straight Arrow
Ranch—the largest spread in these parts—ever since.

For kids and kisses, tears and laughter, wild horses and wilder men—
come to the Straight Arrow Ranch, near Cupid, Colorado. Come meet
the Camerons.

THE CAMERONS OF COLORADO
by Ruth Jean Dale

Kids, Critters and Cupid (Superromance#678)
available in February 1996

The Cupid Conspiracy (Temptation #579)
available in March 1996

The Cupid Chronicles (Superromance #687)
available in April 1996

JASMINE CRESSWELL

Bestselling author Jasmine Cresswell makes her
Temptation debut in February 1996 with #574
MIDNIGHT FANTASY. Heroine Ariel Hutton
secretly longed for adventure and excitement in
her life. Getting kidnapped by sexy, mysterious
Mac was a start! Except Mac was *not* quite what
he appeared to be....

Upcoming books by Jasmine Cresswell:

—*Weddings by DeWilde* series
SHATTERED VOWS (April 1996)
I DO, AGAIN (March 1997)

—MIRA books
NO SIN TOO GREAT (May 1996)
CHARADES (June 1996)
Look for these titles at your local bookstore!